The Choices We Make

Rhonda Faye Crumpton

PublishAmerica
Baltimore

First printing

ISBN: 1-4137-5529-1
PUBLISHED BY PUBLISHAMERICA, LLLP
www.publishamerica.com
Baltimore

Printed in the United States of America

In loving memory of my father, John Perry Crumpton, and Pamela Williams Baker, who inspired me to write my first play.

And in honor of my children and grandchildren, Sherise, Alisa, Travis, Travis Jr. and Tionne J'ohnae; my honorary son, Jay Sumpter; and my mother, Mary Crumpton.

Acknowledgments

If I were to recognize everyone who has been a positive influence in my life, the acknowledgements would be as long as the book. To my children: Sherise Sanders, Alisa Sanders, and Travis Leach, I just want to say I love you all. To my grandchildren (who can't read yet), you are my jewels.

I want to recognize "the chain of command," the rest of my family: my sister, Karen Martin, and her daughter, Kia; my brother, Bill and his children, Perry and Denise; the other two people who made it possible for me to be a Grandmother, Pamela Blakeley and Ralph Reed, Jr.; and our special family friend, Joe Berryman. Also to my aunt and uncle and cousins, The Lynn Petty Family, my Goddaughter, Nonya Brown and her family, and all of my other cousins.

All scripture reference is based on Today's English Version of the Good News Bible published by Thomas Nelson, Inc.

I want to give a special shout out and love to my pastor, Rev. Mamie L. Wilson and to my Blandonia church family. I give a shout out to my Sunday school class, especially to Shelia Petty, Karen Creacy, Sarah Raeford, and to the Gospel Choir.

I give a shout out to all the pastors and first ladies in the Sanford, North Carolina area, especially to Bishop Charles and Pastor Patti Melette because people could not understand why they built their church where they did, but now they see the vision. To Pastor Steve Chesney and his wife, Tonya, if this book is ever made into a movie you two have to provide the singing voices.

Also to my cousins and their spouses who pastor churches, Dr. Lewis and Pastor Alice Hooker, and Pastor Nathane and First Lady Donna Hooker.

To my friends, Pastor Hugh McLean and his wife Melissa, and to Minister Delisa Williams, thank you for all the encouragement. I give a shout out to all of my friends, but especially to those who have been my friends since grade school: Reba, Paula, Marshal, Cynthia, and especially to Chip Knotts, my confidante over the years.

Making the Right Choices is based on a play I wrote back in 2000. To write the novel I had to think of real people and places and change them up some to get my imagination going. I imagined Levi living in the house where the Beady Waddell Family lived back in the day, and Shalan living in the house where I grew up with Mrs. Frances Bethea living between us. Mother Ingram originally had only one son but, for the book, I gave her two more in honor of the three fine sons that my Godparents, Doyle and Josephine Turner, raised.

A special thank you to Jonah Jones and Ralph Reed, Jr. who acted as sounding boards.

I send a special shout out to Elaine's Restaurant, Donna's Hair Salon, Reggie Creacy of We Do Photos, Knotts Funeral Home, and CCCC, all in Sanford.

Prologue

Perry Ingram opened the door to his mother's house and called out to her, "Mom, we're here." The doctor had recently advised Mrs. Ingram, or Mother Ingram as she was called at the church, to have someone move in with her. Perry had offered to let her come stay with him and his family, but she wouldn't hear of it. As much as she loved her daughter-in-law and was loved in return, she knew she was set in her ways. She was used to running her own household, being in her own kitchen. She didn't want to do anything to make her daughter-in-law uncomfortable in her own home. Besides, this was the house her late husband had brought her to as a bride. They had raised three boys here and she wasn't ready to let go of the memories.

Perry, her youngest son, and the only one still living in the area, had come up with the suggestion that she find a live-in companion to do light housekeeping in exchange for room and board. She didn't need 'round the clock care, just someone to be there some of the time. Earlier in the year, around the same time her husband, Sylvester, had gone home to be with the Lord, Mother Ingram had been diagnosed with diabetes. Although she had a lot of faith in the Lord, she sometimes found herself weeping and depressed. Some nights Perry and Mary or one of their children stayed over because Mother Ingram had never lived alone in all of her 78 years, and the adjustment had been very difficult for her.

"Hey, Mama." Perry greeted her with a kiss on the cheek as she entered the living room. "This is Shalan Sanders that I was telling you about, and this is her son, Kendrick." The two women greeted one another as Kendrick peeped shyly around his mother.

"And how are you, Kendrick?" Mother Ingram bent down to greet the cute little boy with the big, light brown eyes.

"Fine, thank you," he replied in a low voice.

Mother Ingram gave him a smile and straightened up. She knew he would warm up to her in no time. She again addressed Shalan, "Where are your bags?"

"Well as I was telling your son, I didn't want to move in until you had a chance to meet us. Are you sure having a young child around won't bother you?"

"Nonsense, I raised three boys in this old house. Kendrick, you can even call me Grandmother Ingram if you want to. Shalan, you go get your bags and check out of that motel right now. You're doing me a favor."

"We're doing each other a favor. We just moved here and all the decent apartments are so expensive. Here Kendrick will have a nice yard to play in."

"Have you found a job yet and someone to look after Kendrick?"

"Yes, ma'am. I'll be working as a receptionist at the hospital. I enrolled Kendrick in preschool today, but he'll be going to daycare until it starts."

"Unless you just want him in daycare all day, he could come here on your lunch hour. He would be a lot of company for me. I could have lunch ready and the three of us could eat together. Then when he gets used to me, I could pick him up and you wouldn't have to come home unless you wanted to."

"Oh, Mother Ingram, I couldn't possibly ask you to do all of that. I already feel like I'm getting the best part of the deal."

"Nonsense. He'll probably sleep a couple of hours after lunch anyway. Of course I don't want to pressure you. You do what you think is best."

Shalan looked at Mother Ingram and could tell that she would really love having Kendrick and was not simply being polite. "Thank you, Mrs. Ingram, I would love having Kendrick stay here with you. We'll be back in a couple of hours."

"Okay, baby, and you can just call me Mother Ingram. Everybody does."

"All right. Let me just tell Mr. Ingram we're leaving. I followed him over here."

"Don't you need help getting your bags?"

"No, we can manage. I'll see you in a little while."

In the days and weeks that followed, Shalan and Kendrick settled into a comfortable routine at Mother Ingram's. Shalan cooked breakfast each day and did most of the weekend cooking. True to her word, Mother Ingram had a light lunch prepared each day when Shalan brought Kendrick home. Since Kendrick ate at the daycare, he usually just sat at the table with them and talked about his morning. After a couple of weeks, Shalan started eating with the new friends she was making at work. She came straight home each day after work and sat down to the delicious meal Mother Ingram had ready. She and Kendrick would always spend time outdoors after eating.

Kendrick seemed to thrive in his new environment. He followed Mother Ingram around, chattering away. Perry's newly married son, Travis, and his wife, Kara, came over sometimes and took him to the park or to the zoo. "We're practicing," they always assured Shalan when she worried if Kendrick was being a bother. "Besides, Kendrick is so sweet, how could he worry us?" Kendrick would look at her with his sweet innocent look that made him look so much like his dad, that Shalan's heart would melt as she kissed him goodbye and sent him with the younger Ingrams.

Shalan and Mother Ingram developed a genuine love for one another. Shalan's grandmother, her dad's mom, had passed when she was 10 years old. Her other three grandparents had died before she was born, so this was a new experience having the older woman to confide in. Some nights after Kendrick was sleep, Mother Ingram would tell her about her marriage to Sylvester. They had been high school sweethearts and had been married for 61 years. Her eyes would take on a misty, faraway look as she reminisced. Shalan knew without being told that Mother Ingram still loved her husband, though death separated them. One night she looked thoughtfully at Shalan and asked her about Kendrick's father.

"He was a good friend. One night we just took our friendship to another level. It was a one time thing." Although Shalan spoke in a matter of fact way, Mother Ingram could sense the hurt behind her simple words.

"What did he say when you told him you were pregnant?" After a long pause, Shalan replied that she never told him.

"Telling him would have changed the course of his life. I lo… I thought too much of our friendship to do that."

"But if he was such a good friend, surely he questioned your pregnancy? Didn't your mama and daddy insist you tell him?"

"The same weekend I got pregnant, Mama and Daddy had gone to Florida with another couple. On the way back a transfer truck hit them and all four of them were killed instantly."

"Oh, honey, I'm so sorry. I didn't know your folks were dead! You never mentioned it." Mother Ingram had thought it strange that Shalan never mentioned her parents, but had assumed there was some sort of estrangement. Not wanting to pry, she had waited for Shalan to bring them up.

"I know. It still hurts to talk about them sometimes." Shalan looked down to hide the glisten of tears in her eyes. "As a matter of fact, Kendrick's grandparents were supposed to go with them that weekend, but his youngest sister had won the local oratorical contest and had to compete on the district level that same weekend. The other couple took their place."

"If the families were that close, I'm sure they would like to know they have a grandson."

"Yeah, I know in hindsight I should have said something. Especially now that Kendrick's at the age where he's asking questions."

"You still love him, don't you?" she asked gently. A denial sprang to Shalan's lips, but it died as quickly as it had sprung to life.

"Yes," she admitted, "but I'm ready to move on with my life."

"And you should, but you know in your heart you have some wrongs to right. I know you were young and having just lost your parents, I know you weren't thinking straight. But now you're older and you've accepted Christ in your life. You know what you need to do."

"But what if he's married by now? I haven't been in touch with him in years."

"But you know how to get in touch with his family?"

"Yes, but I haven't talked to them either."

"We're going to pray about the situation and let God direct you. He's going to work everything out. Just wait and see. Now let's pray." Together the two women kneeled on either side of the coffee table, joining hands across the table. Mother Ingram began to pray. "Father, in the name of Jesus, we come before You right now because you know all things. Father, You are the Author and the Finisher of our faith. Now, Lord, we have a situation here, a situation that may change Shalan's life and her son's life. And, Lord, it might change the life of a young man that I've never met. But You know him. You know all about him. In Your time, we need Your help in making things right. Lord, do it in such a way that Shalan will know that it was Your hand that did the directing. Lord, we're asking for a miracle, in the name of Jesus, and we thank you in advance. Oh yeah, God, I feel Your presence right now. Ooh, I thank You."

Tears were flowing freely down both women's checks. Shalan lifted her voice in praise as the spirit gave utterance. Both women lifted their hands in praise as they rose to their feet, Shalan first, then Mother Ingram more slowly. Finally as the Spirit died down the two women embraced, weeping unashamedly. "It's going to be all right, baby. Now go get some rest. Tomorrow's a work day."

Chapter 1

Levi Leach looked critically at the neckties he had brought with him, trying to decide which one to wear tonight. He smiled to himself as he thought of the one thing the *new Levi* had in common with the *old Levi.* They both loved to dress to impress.

Rev. Levi Leach, a recent graduate of the Harvey C. Palmer Theological Seminary in Atlanta, Georgia was on the outskirts of Baltimore, Maryland running a revival for a small but dedicated church. One of the officers of the church, Brother Perry Ingram, had heard him in North Carolina when he was preaching for the Search Committee of a church that needed a full-time pastor. The committee had decided to go with an older minister who had some experience under his belt. *An older, married minister,* thought Levi. *Oh well, if Vanessa has her way, I'll soon be a married man myself. But how can a brother get experience if no one hires him?* There had been one offer, but it just hadn't seemed a comfortable fit to Levi. He had decided to work for a temporary agency and wait a couple of months before circulating his PIF (Personal Information Form). As he finished putting on his 100% silk purple tie, the phone rang. "Hello?"

"Hi, baby." Levi smiled as he heard Linda Leach's voice cross the miles to him from Sanford, North Carolina, his hometown.

"Hey, Momma!"

"How's the revival going?" Although Linda and Will had six children, they took an interest in what each one was doing. There had been little sibling rivalry in the Leach household because each child was made to feel special.

"Okay, I guess. We had more of a crowd last night than Monday and Tuesday."

"I guess word is getting around about how my baby can preach!"

"Aw, Momma, you know I give God all the glory. It's not even about me. I do think they want me to stay and pastor their church, though."

"That's good news; you don't sound too excited."

"It's not that. I believe I have the heart of a pastor, I really do, but..." his voice trailed off as he tried to put his thoughts into words that would fool his mother, not an easy thing to do.

"But what?"

"Two things. One, this church is in the heart of drug city and I don't know what else. This will be my first church, Momma. I just don't know if I can handle the problems that are bound to come up."

"You mentioned two things. What's the other thing?"

"I met a man at the motel restaurant last night. His church is looking for a full-time pastor. The way he described the benefits sound too good to be true. I rode by and looked at the church and it was awesome! I'm trying to pump myself up for tonight's service, but I just keep seeing that other church. And thinking about how much sooner I can pay off my student loans if I accept this other job."

"And what is the Lord saying about all of this?"

"Well, nothing yet." Levi had known this was coming.

"Meaning you haven't gotten an answer or you haven't bothered to pray about it?" There was a significant pause. When Levi remained silent, Linda continued. "You listen to me, Levi, and you listen good. I know you're a grown man, even though I still call you and all my children baby, but you need to remember that you're also a man of God. You've been set apart a long time for such a time as this. You don't go into any situation without talking to your Father about it first. And I'm not talking about your daddy either. Yeah you listen to what both churches have to offer, but then, son, you'd better lay before the Lord. Let Him lead you. He's not going to lead you anywhere that His grace can't keep you."

"I hear you, Momma. I guess I need to wait until I have an offer before I start worrying the Lord about the situation anyway. Neither of the churches has said anything definite. Mr. McKoy invited me to have lunch with some of the officers of his church tomorrow."

"Is he the man you met at the restaurant?"

"Yes, ma'am."

"Well, Levi, as much as I'm enjoying talking to you, I think you need to hang up now and try to focus on tonight. This might be somebody's night to find salvation, and you don't want to be up there with a bunch of mess on your mind."

"Okay, Momma. You're right, I love you."

"I love you, too. You have a good night."

"You, too, Momma. Be blessed." As he hung up, Levi felt the urge to pray. "Father, sometimes the old me wants to rise up and I get caught up in self, but Lord I know that if I confess my faults, You are mighty and just to forgive. Jesus, I don't want anything to hinder me tonight. Just use me for your glory. Let some man or woman, boy or girl, have a life-changing experience tonight. Lord, You did it for me, I know You can do it for others. Lord, I just die from myself right now. Let the mighty warrior in me stand up." As he began to praise God, the Spirit began to make intercession. He didn't know, but wouldn't have been surprised to know, that in North Carolina, his mother was praying for tonight's revival, as well.

Chapter 2

Levi walked into the restaurant and looked around. Mr. McKoy noticed him and waved him over. "Rev. Leach, so good to see you again." They shook hands and Levi was introduced to the other men at the table. "This is Mr. Williams, Mr. Lyles, and Mr. Martin." Levi greeted each man, careful to make eye contact. Mr. McKoy seemed to be the designated spokesperson for the group, which made sense, Levi supposed, since he had set the meeting up. "We caught part of the service last night."

"I thought I saw you near the back, but after service I didn't see you so I wasn't sure."

"Yeah, we eased out. The service got a little too long there at the end. All of those people going up for prayer. When will people realize they can pray for themselves?" Levi was saved from having to answer when the waitress came over. Before he could look at the offered menu, Mr. Williams broke his silence and announced they would all take the special. He did give Levi the courtesy of letting him order his own drink.

"Do you have lemonade?" Levi asked the waitress, wondering if he should get water since this appeared to be a budget lunch.

Mr. McKoy continued. "Our services are a little different from the one you were in last night."

"A *little* different?" asked Mr. Lyles with a snort.

"Well a lot different," Mr. McKoy allowed. "Now if I'm correct, you've never pastored a church before, is that right?"

"No, I haven't." He was sure that he had said as much to Mr. McKoy when they first met.

"But you have been to a seminary?"

"Yes, sir."

Mr. Martin spoke up. "We can probably work with you then. We offer a good salary. You don't have to worry about rent or utilities. There's a beautiful manse right beside the church. And don't think our members will be coming over there worrying you all the time either. No siree. We adhere to your schedule. You'll have office hours at the church. Of course now if someone has an emergency, we expect you to be available."

Levi simply nodded. "Are you married, son?" This from Mr. Williams.

"No, I'm not."

"Engaged?" he pressed.

"Not officially. I've been seeing someone and I guess that's the direction we're headed."

Mr. McKoy regained control as the spokesman. "Good, we need you married. A single, young pastor, decent looking like yourself, man, I can't tell you how many women will be wanting to join the church and causing trouble."

Not to be outdone, Mr. Martin added his two cents. "Now, Reverend, we know you're a man of God and everything, but we also know you're a man. We just ask that you be discreet."

"Pardon?" Levi had to wait on an answer because the waitress arrived with their food. Levi glanced at his plate to see that the special included meat loaf, mashed potatoes and gravy, green beans and rolls. Luckily, it was food that he liked.

"As I was saying," Mr. Martin continued, "if you want to be with some gal just don't have her at the manse. You know what I'm saying."

With the exception of Levi, they all had a good chuckle. "Men will be men," interjected Mr. Williams. "Where does your fiancee live?"

"She's not actually my fiancee, but she lives in Atlanta. I met her when I was in school. And as far as entertaining women in the way you're suggesting, that won't be a problem at all."

Mr. McKoy said, "Oh well, we'll see." The men got another good chuckle. After a few bites, he asked Levi if he had been looking at any other churches. He replied that while he didn't have a formal offer, he thought Christ's Church might offer him a position.

"You aren't talking about where we were last night, I hope?" Mr. Lyles asked incredulously.

"Yes," Levi stated simply with no elaboration.

Mr. McKoy held up a hand to Mr. Lyles as if to say, *Let me handle this*. Then to Levi, "Boy, you're too bright to get suckered into something like that. That's for someone who has no options. The only thing we would ask is to cut your sermon a little bit. After 20 minutes people's attention wanders anyway. We're going to pay you the same thing for a 15 or 20- minute sermon as we are for a 45-minute sermon so you may as well save your energy. Make sense?"

Mr. Williams added, "Those people will have you at their beck and call 24/7 and probably for a fourth of what we're going to give you."

"Well like I said, they haven't offered me the job yet. It's just a feeling I have," Levi said while thinking, *45 minutes? Come on, I know it wasn't that long.*

"So can you come preach for us Sunday so the rest of the congregation can hear you?" asked Mr. McKoy.

"Yes, I had planned to leave Sunday morning, but I can change to an afternoon flight."

"Good, be there at 10:45, we start right at 11:00, we should be out by 12, no later than 12:15. We'll even drive you to the airport."

"No, thanks anyway, but I have a rental car I need to turn in. Well, if you gentlemen will excuse me, I have some more studying to do."

"I thought you said you had graduated already," said Mr. McKoy.

"I have, but I meant studying for tonight's message."

"Oh, oh yeah, right, right." Levi was not quite out of hearing distance when he heard Mr. McKoy state that he was a little strange, but he had potential. There was a murmur of agreement before the conversation turned to dessert.

As he stepped outside the restaurant, Levi looked up. "Lord, You know You're going to have to help a brother out." As he unlocked the door to his room at the Holiday Inn Express where he was staying this week, the telephone was ringing. It had to be either his mother or his girlfriend, Vanessa. "Hello?"

"Hello, sweetheart." *Vanessa,* he thought without the joy he should have felt. He sat on the bed and starting loosening his tie. "Hi, honey, how are you?"

"I'm fine, but you should be asking *where* am I?"

"Okay, I'll bite. Where are you?"

"Downstairs in the lobby. You just walked right past me."

"What! What are you doing here?"

"I came to support, what else? And guess who came with me?"

"Who?" *Please, Jesus, don't let it be who I think it is.*

"Mother and Father are with me!"

Oh, man, this day was definitely going downhill. What next?

"Levi? Are you there?"

"I'll be right down," he said with as much enthusiasm as he could muster.

Chapter 3

Mother Ingram had been under the weather all week. Revival had been going on at the church and she hadn't been there a single night. Shalan had stayed home with her despite her protests. She was determined to go tomorrow since it was the last night. Perry and Mary had been telling them how anointed the young man of God was that was running the revival. As she, Kendrick, and Shalan sat at the kitchen table after finishing dinner, they heard Perry call out from the living room. "Back here," she called.

Mary and Perry came inside the kitchen. "We were just stopping by to see if you were up to going to church tonight," Mary told her.

"No, but I'm going to press my way tomorrow night, no matter what. But why don't you take Shalan with you? There's no reason why she shouldn't go; I'm feeling a lot better."

"Oh, no," Shalan protested. "I'll just wait and go with you tomorrow night. I hate to leave you here by yourself."

"No, you go on." Mother Ingram insisted.

"Look, why don't I stay here with you?" Mary offered. "I've been all week and I know Shalan will enjoy herself more if she knows I'm here with you."

"Really there's no need for anybody to stay. All of you go on and don't worry about me."

"I want to go to church, Mama," said Kendrick.

"Okay, baby, we'll go. Miss Mary, are you going to stay here?"

"No," said Mother Ingram before Mary could answer.

"I guess not." Mary smiled. "You two go on and get ready. We'll wait for you."

"I'll just drive then you two won't have to drop us off." As Shalan got herself and Kendrick ready, she thought about how happy she was with her new church. A lot of the members had stopped coming when the previous pastor retired, and the congregation was having trouble recruiting someone to fill the pulpit. The officers of the church spoke some Sundays and guest preachers came on the other Sundays. She knew from talking to Perry that a lot of the remaining members were hoping that the preacher doing the revival would consider staying. Rev. Leak, the announcement had read in Sunday's bulletin, which made her think of her old friend Levi Leach and wonder how he was doing, and if he went by *Rev*. Leach these days.

Shalan had gotten involved in church life right away. She sang with the gospel choir and helped with the youth choir. She and Kendrick had joined the Sunday school and she attended Bible study each week. Kara, Mother Ingram's granddaughter-in-law had even tried to fix her up with the minister of music. They had gone out a couple of times but realized there was no future for them other than friendship. She wanted to take some time to get settled before she got seriously involved. That was the reason she told everyone, but her heart mocked her.

"Exactly what are you looking for in a man?" Kara had asked her.

"I want a man who loves God, who loves me, someone who will love my son as if he were his own. I want someone I can pray with, cry with, laugh with, and...

"And?" Kara prompted.

"Who makes me blush," Shalan had answered, hoping she didn't sound too silly. Now as she helped Kendrick out of the car and followed Perry and Mary up the church steps, she was thinking only about hearing a word from the Lord.

"Oh, Shalan, I knew there was something I meant to ask you," said Perry. "When you mention Sanford, I always think about Florida, but you told me earlier you were from North Carolina, didn't you?"

"Yes, sir, Sanford, North Carolina. Why?"

"That's where Rev. Leach is from!"

"Rev. Leach?" Shalan's mouth had suddenly gone dry.

"Yes. Come on back and say hello. You probably know him. He's not that much older than you."

"Yes, I do know some Leaches from Sanford, but I wouldn't dare go in now. He's probably praying or something."

"Well, wait here and I'll go see. It might do him good to know a familiar face is in the congregation."

Shalan looked around for a way out, but she knew she was going to have to face Levi eventually. She looked around for Mary, but didn't see her anywhere. Maybe if he couldn't see her now, she could sneak out before the benediction and say that Kendrick had gotten sleepy and…

"Shalan, go on in. I've got to make sure the mikes are set up." Perry smiled at her waiting for her to take the few steps that would bring her face to face with Levi. Her heart felt like it was going to burst.

"Mommy, what's wrong?" questioned Kendrick. Shalan realized that she had been squeezing his little hand.

"Nothing, baby, nothing. We're just going to go say hello to the preacher. Then we'll go sit down."

"Hi, Levi, long time no see." Shalan tried to speak calmly, but she heard the quiver in her voice.

"Shalan! What are you doing here?"

"I'm just here to hear the Word like everyone else."

"Yeah, and what Word is that? You want to see what kind of preacher I turned out to be? You turned your back on our friendship like it was nothing and then you just sashay up in here like it's nothing. Don't tell me you're one of those women who want to hook up with a preacher?" For the first time, he noticed Kendrick looking at him with wide, frightened eyes. "Is he yours?"

"Yes," answered Shalan shortly.

Levi lowered his voice, sensing that he had frightened Shalan's son. "Look, Shalan, I'm a man of God. I'm about to go out there and preach His word. I don't need this right now. On top of everything else, my soon to be fiancee and her parents are out there. Just leave me a number where you can be reached, and I'll be in touch."

Shalan was so humiliated and furious that she was shaking. "You are so full of yourself! I wouldn't stay and hear you preach if I never heard preaching again! Brother Ingram just thought I should say hello to an old friend from my hometown. But I guess that friend doesn't exist anymore, because the Levi Leach I knew wouldn't talk like that to anyone even before he was saved! Excuse us, your Excellency, for taking up your holy time. Come on, baby." With her hand on the doorknob, Shalan turned around for one parting shot. "I understand now why the Bible says to know those who labor among you."

Shalan's only thought was reaching her car before she broke down in tears. She passed Perry on her way out. He couldn't help but notice her distress, but only nodded when she insisted she was okay. He debated on following her to her car or confronting the preacher. He decided to confront the preacher. He knew he had made an error in judgement by disturbing the man of God before he preached. But if Shalan's face was any indication, maybe he'd better see what shape the preacher was in before he stood before the congregation.

Levi was in shock to say the least! How could he have spoken so harshly to someone who had been his best friend? He couldn't believe how ignorant he had acted. Shalan, a mother! A jealousy like he had never known rushed through his body. There was a light knock on the study door.

"Rev. Leach, I couldn't help but notice how upset Shalan looked. Did I do wrong sending her in here?"

"How did she know I was here?"

"She didn't until five minutes ago. She's a live-in companion to my mother. The only reason she hasn't been this week is that my mother's been sick. This is Shalan's church."

"Oh, man, did I blow it! I accused her of man hunting. She must think I'm a fool."

Before he thought about what he was saying, Perry responded, "I kind of think so myself if you snubbed a sweet young woman like Shalan. I tried to introduce myself to your girlfriend just now and welcome her to the church, but she wasn't having it. She did manage to tell me you two are engaged."

"We aren't officially engaged, and she's not snooty. You just have to get to know her."

"Yeah, I see," Perry replied doubtfully. "Anyway, I hope you will apologize to Shalan before you leave town."

"I will, Brother Ingram. I will."

"I don't mind telling you, Rev. Leach, we think a lot of you. We're even thinking about asking you to be our Pastor. But like I said, Shalan is a part of this church and a part of my family as well. I won't see her mistreated by you or by anyone else."

"Shalan used to be the very best friend I had in the world. She hurt me, though, by moving away and not even telling me. I guess the flesh just wanted to hurt back."

"I understand; we'll talk later. Again, I apologize. I should have let you have this time to yourself. The Praise Team is singing now so I'm going to leave you and let you get yourself together."

"All right, thank you." Levi walked over and locked the door to make sure he wasn't disturbed. He hoped the Praise Team had a lot to praise Him for, because he had some serious praying to do. "Lord, I don't want to get puffed up with pride. God, forgive me, please forgive me! Lord, when I saw her I remembered how she just walked out of my life before I could tell her I loved her. It hurt back then, Lord, and I just wanted to hurt her tonight. But, Lord, I'm supposed to be above such pettiness. Oh, God, I repent. Continue to use me, Lord. Don't take your Holy Spirit from me. Give me a fresh anointing. God give me a word for your people tonight. Lord, cause souls to be saved. Let those who are in captivity be set free, loose those who are bound, Lord, heal the sick. Comfort the broken hearted. Lord, I die from myself right now. Let this flesh be silenced so that Your glory can shine through. In the name of Jesus, I pray." Before he could say Amen, the Spirit began to give utterance and he let Him have his way.

An anointing had come on Levi, as he had never felt before. While he was preaching, it was like someone else was doing the work and he was an observer. "In closing, my brothers and sisters, I'd like to ask you this question. Do you have the spirit of Paul or of Saul? Even after Paul's conversion, I can imagine that Saul still wanted to be a big part of the picture. He no doubt tried to remind Paul that he had been educated by the best and that he could go anywhere and be anything he wanted to be. I can imagine Saul telling the new creature Paul, 'You don't have to persecute Christians anymore, but I don't see why a man with your education and background allows himself to put up with such abuse. Why suffer the indignities of being shipwrecked and beaten and thrown in prison? Man, is it worth it?' And I can imagine Paul stepping to Saul and saying, 'Anything that I have to do to bring souls to Christ, that's what I'll do. Saul, you're dead to me. Jesus has created a new me. I'm forgetting those things that are behind me and pressing toward the mark of the high calling, which is in Jesus. Depart from me.'

"So it is my brothers and sisters, sometimes the old you will rear up and try to accuse God. The old you will try to convince the new you that the price is too high to follow Jesus. Are you yielding to that voice? Or are you listening to the Shepherd? He tells us that His sheep hear His voice. While the choir sings, I invite anyone saved or unsaved to meet me at the altar. If you have not totally surrendered to the calling that God has on your life, let this be your night. Don't put if off another day. And I want to be the first at the altar because this week has been for me as well as for anybody. I've found myself trying to run God's business. But tonight, Church, I'm putting it all in His hands. Whatever He requires of me, that will I do. Hallelujah! If it costs my life, Church, I want to do His will!" Levi cried unashamedly.

The congregation rose to its feet with many crying and others offering up praise.

"If one of the officers of the church will come and pray for me first, I'll pray for anyone who needs prayer. Won't you come? Sing, choir."

As Perry and one of the other brothers of the church prayed for Levi, practically the entire church stood waiting at the altar. Vanessa and her parents sat looking neither to the right nor to the left.

"When did he get so Pentecostal acting?" Mrs. Lamar whispered to Vanessa.

"I don't know, but you can believe I'm going to have a long talk with him. This is so embarrassing."

"Let's just tip out," Rev. Lamar said, "although with all of this noise I don't think we have to tip." The three of them left and went to a local Waffle House to give Levi time to get back to the motel. "You be sure to encourage him to take that job Brother McKoy offered him and don't let him know I set it up."

"Okay, Daddy."

"And for God's sake, try to talk to him about being so emotional! Maybe I'll take him out on the golf course Saturday and talk to him a little bit. Yeah, I think that's what I'll do. Don't worry, princess, Daddy'll get to the bottom of this mess."

Chapter 4

As Shalan and Kendrick drove home they listened to the "Donnie McClurkin featuring Marvin Winans" CD. "Mommy, why was that preacher mean to you?"

"He was probably nervous about preaching and took it out on me. He didn't mean to sound like that."

"Preachers shouldn't be mean to people, should they, Mommy?"

"No, baby, but they're people like we are and they make mistakes, too."

"Then what happens? Does God punish them?"

"Well most of the time if they are truly God's children and not just pretending to be, the Holy Spirit will let them know they've done something wrong. Then they have a chance to make it right and get forgiven. Just like when you do something wrong, I give you a chance to make it right."

"Are you going to forgive him if he tries to make it right?"

"Of course, honey, because if I didn't forgive him, then God wouldn't be pleased with me." *But he can forget about me telling him that you're his son.*

"Oh."

Mother Ingram was just getting off the couch to go to her bedroom when she heard a car pull up. *Now who can that be?* she wondered. Shalan and Kendrick came in. She could see the tenseness on Shalan's face and wisely didn't ask what was wrong in front of Kendrick. "Why don't you get Kendrick ready for bed then come down for a minute?"

"All right. Tell Grandmother Ingram good night, Kendrick."

"Goodnight. The preacher was mean to my mommy."

Mother Ingram looked at Shalan for a denial; when none was forthcoming, she kissed Kendrick and went to put the coffee on. She had a feeling this would be a late night.

"How are you feeling, Mother Ingram?" Shalan had come quietly into the kitchen.

"Just tell me."

The tears that Shalan had been holding inside burst forth.

"That's right. Get it out." She walked over to the younger woman and held her as she cried as though her heart would break.

Finally, in halting words, she was able to speak. "He thought I was there to make trouble for him, that I was on the prowl looking for a man."

"But why would he think such a thing? You can trust me. Anything you and I talk about in this house stays in this house. You know that."

"Yes, ma'am, I know. He used to be a friend of mine, my best friend. But I didn't know he was the one running the revival until we got there. Mr. Perry told me to go in the study and say hello. But he acted so different, so conceited... Kendrick and I just left."

"He's Kendrick's father, isn't he?" Mother Ingram had to strain to hear Shalan's simple, soft answer.

"Yes."

"And when you saw him, was the love still there?"

Shalan could only nod as she tried to hold back another flood of tears. Long into the night she shared her fondest memories of her friendship with the Leach family.

Chapter 5

The Past

For as long as she could remember, Shalan Sanders had lived one house up from the Leach family. It was a good thing that Miss Frances, who lived between them, was such a sweet lady because they often used her yard as a shortcut. There were six children in the Leach household and although Shalan was in the class with Hugh, she and Levi were closer. Levi was two years older, and over the years, he and Shalan had become best friends. Shalan knew every girl that Levi had ever liked. He confided in her more than he did to any of the guys he hung around.

The two things about Levi that exasperated Shalan to no end were first, his unsolicited advice on her love life, or her social life, since she had never considered herself in love. Every time she had a date, before her date could even get settled in the living room, there was Levi at the door. You would think he was her father the way he grilled the guy on what movie they were going to see or which of the two clubs that teens in their town frequented they were going to. Guys used to comment on how protective her "cousin" was of her. At first Shalan corrected them on the relationship, telling them they were not related. She soon found out it was best to leave well enough alone, however. Once they found out he wasn't related they gave her the "look." The "now I know why you don't want to get serious about anyone" look.

Levi would always ask how her date went, then proceed to tell her why he didn't think that particular guy was right for her. The reasons ranged all the way to "He's a playa, out for one thing" to "He looks a little too sweet to me." When he couldn't find anything wrong with them his comment was usually, "He's a'right, but y'all are too much alike to get along."

The second drawback to her friendship with Levi, which wasn't his fault, was his looks. Levi was "all of that"—tall, handsome, athletic, charismatic. Because she had known him since she was three, Shalan never paid his good looks any attention. That is until she and Hugh went to high school. Once girls found out Hugh was Levi's brother, and Shalan his best friend, everyone wanted a hook up. "Girl, you just got to invite me over to your house, does he live right next door?" or "Why don't you have a party so I can meet him?" Shalan appreciated those who were honest about their intentions more so than those who never even spoke to her in class, but just *had to* talk to her when they saw her with Levi at lunch or after school.

Levi usually looked on with amusement during these thinly veiled conversations. For the most part, he only went out with the girls in his class. Every three or four months he would date one girl exclusively. As soon as everyone thought that one would be the one, he would gradually stop seeing her. Shalan liked the times in between Levi's girlfriends because he would hang with her, Hugh, and their younger sister, Angie. Some weekends they would just hang out at one of their houses and listen to music or watch movies. Some nights they would go to one of the clubs.

One night they were at the *Shangri-La Club* where a live band was performing. The lead singer held up a $100 bill and challenged anyone to come on stage and imitate any artist living or dead. "Come on, male or female, my band knows all the hits. The winner will receive this crisp, new $100 bill. Come on now, I know somebody out there can sing. I know you can't sing like me, ya know what I'm saying, but if you can sing a little bit, come on up. Tell you what I'm even going to give the runner up $50."

"Man, he thinks he's all that," said Levi. "If I went up there, I'd make *him* sit down."

"Yeah, right," Shalan and Angie said almost in unison.

"I ain't ever heard you sing," said Shalan.

"That's what I'm talking about," said Angie, "and I live with him. Hugh, have you heard him sing?"

"No, but if he sings as loud as he snores, he better back up from the mike." While they were having their little discussion, a girl had gone up and said she was going to do "Ain't No Mountain High Enough" by Diana Ross. Three guys got up and then, to his siblings' and friend's amazement, Levi got up, too.

"Okay, we'll let the lady go first. Guys pick a letter out of that box over there. Whoever has the letter closest to *A* goes first. Okay, little lady, what's your name?"

"Aretha."

"Aretha? You gotta be kidding! You need to be singing about some RESPECT instead of about some mountain. But okay, do your thang." Aretha had a sweet voice and stayed on key. She was nothing to write home about, but pleasant to listen to. She got a round of applause and no heckling from the audience.

"Okay, who do we have up next?" Levi stepped up. "Tell us what you're going to sing."

"Still Waters Run Deep."

"A Four Tops hit. Man, you kids are reaching way back. Your parents must have you listening to the oldies. That's all right, I ain't mad at 'cha. And I guess your name is Levi Stubbs?"

"Actually it *is* Levi—Levi Leach." With that, Levi took the microphone, walked coolly off the stage and came closer to his audience. The whole place was hushed as he sang. Tears streamed down Shalan's face. She tried to wipe them before anyone could see, but as she glanced at Angie, she saw that she was just as emotional. Hugh just sat with an amazed look on his face. The other three contestants left the stage and took their seats without performing. Levi finished, handed the mike back to the lead singer of the band, and went to stand beside Aretha.

For the space of a few seconds, the lead singer was speechless. Then, as if in a daze, he went to Aretha. "By your applause." There was a polite round of applause. He stepped on the other side of Levi. "By your applause." The roar was deafening, the crowd on its feet. "And we have our winner."

Levi came back to his seat as if nothing out of the ordinary had happened. Later, on the way home, everybody was talking at once.

"Why is it no one knew you could sing, man?"

"I sing in the choir with you guys every fourth Sunday. Would I be in the choir if I couldn't sing? On second thought, don't answer that, 'cause Hugh is in the choir and I've heard him try to sing."

"But you never lead any songs," Shalan protested.

"I've never been *asked* to lead any songs. And please, don't go spreading this around 'cause I'm not trying to get up there every time somebody needs a free soloist at a funeral or a wedding. You know how people can make you wish you weren't talented sometimes."

"Nobody in our family can sing like that," said Angie.

"That's because I was kidnapped," said Levi. "Levi Stubbs is my real daddy. He wanted Momma and Daddy to keep me while he was touring with The Four Tops. When he came back, they had run off with me."

"Yeah, right. If anything he paid them to run off with you."

"He probably saw how much you looked like Mr. Leach and decided he needed to raise you," Shalan added just as Levi pulled up in her driveway.

"See you in church tomorrow. Go straight to bed, you know it's our Sunday to sing, and you, my dear, have a solo."

"Okay, dad, see you in the morning."

"That's right. You know I'm your real daddy. Go ask your mama."

"Okay, I think I will."

"Do, and I'll kill you."

Chapter 6

The next morning in church Shalan walked over to Levi in the choir room. "I didn't sleep much last night."

"Because?"

"I was thinking about the talent you're hiding. I'm going to tell Ms. Shelia to let you sing a solo today. I won't even feel right holding that mike knowing how you can sing."

"Look, I love you like a sister, but if you say anything about last night, it's on. I know I've got talent and I give props to the Man Upstairs, but hey, it's different getting up in a club singing and doing it here at church. I don't think I could do it. Maybe one day, but let me decide that, okay?"

Shalan remained stubbornly silent. "What's that? I didn't hear you." Levi folded his arms and looked at her until she reluctantly agreed.

Shalan was sitting on Miss Frances' porch swing one unseasonably warm day in February of Levi's senior year. She saw Levi run out of his house and sprint across the lawn toward her house. "Looking for someone?" she teased as he ran right past her.

"Yeah, I just saw your daddy leave and I was going to check on your moms."

"Oh, okay. MOM," she yelled. Miss Frances and Nancy Sanders stepped out on the porch as Shalan gave Levi a smirk.

"What?"

"Levi wanted to see you," Shalan answered innocently.

"How y'all doing?" Levi went over and hugged both ladies. "I just wanted to share my good news. I just got my acceptance letter from Howard University!"

"I am so proud of you, Levi," said Nancy, giving him a light hug.

"Howard's in DC, isn't it?" asked Miss Frances.

"Yes," answered Shalan. "Levi, you didn't tell me you applied to Howard! Why are you going way up there?"

"It's not way up there. It's about a five-hour drive. I'll probably be home once a month or so." After the two women had gone back in the house, Levi held his hand out to Shalan, indicating they should walk—that was their code for when one of them had something heavy to discuss.

"What?" asked Shalan grumpily.

"Hey, I was going to ask you the same thing. Here I was thinking you would be glad for me and you look like you just lost your best friend." His voice trailed off at the end as realization hit him. "Oh, I see. I'm your best friend, and you're afraid we won't be as close. But, baby, you'll always be my best friend, no matter where I go or who I meet. We're down like that. I was going to tell you alone, but you had to play me like that with your moms. I had to say something. Now stop pouting and give me a hug."

Chapter 7

Shalan and Angie lay on Levi's bed watching him as he finished getting ready for his Senior Prom. "Is there anything called privacy around here?"

"Yeah, I think it's beside your brush."

"You need to hurry up; you're going to be late."

"What after party are you going to?" asked Angie.

"One that's past your curfew."

"Momma already said me and Hugh could stay out until 1:00."

"Momma must have bumped her head because I know she didn't give a freshman, a dumb freshman at that, permission to be out until 1:00. It's bad enough when we let you hang with us in the early night. Okay, how do I look, Shalan?"

"Good, dawg, you look good. Call me when you get home." It was 2:00 a.m. when the phone in Shalan's room rang. She hurriedly picked it up, knowing it would be Levi. "How did it go?"

"So-so."

"Meaning you didn't get your hands in the cookie jar?"

"What do you know about hands in the cookie jar? I'd better not hear tell of anyone putting their hands in *your* cookie jar."

"When am I going to convince you that, number one you're not my daddy, and number two, I'm not a baby? I'm 16 years old!"

"Yeah, you did have a birthday, didn't you? Sweet sixteen and never been kissed."

"Whatever. Just goes to show you don't know everything. So why are you home so early?"

"Man, that girl got drunk as I don't know what! I took her home. I hope her old man doesn't think I got her drunk. Peep this, I went outside with my boys and when I came back inside, homegirl was off the chain!"

"See that's what I've been telling you. If you would go for personality sometimes and not try to date all of these divas, you could find a girlfriend you aren't ashamed to bring home to meet the family."

"You got to admit though, the girl is fine."

"She ain't all of that, now."

"Oh, stop hating."

"Why I gotta be hating, just because I don't see what you see? I'm not supposed to see what you see; I'm a girl. I know one thing, though. You like high yellow girls."

"Ooo, I know you didn't go there. I do not discriminate. I like girls, period."

"Okay, name one brown skinned girlfriend you've had."

"Umm, Reba."

"I rest my case. Reba is one half shade from being high yellow. Look, dawg, I'm going to sleep. I'll holler at you tomorrow. I know you're not coming to church, are you?"

"Yeah, call me when you get up."

"Okay, good night." Just as Shalan fell asleep, the phone rang again. "Yeah?"

"I thought of one," Levi said proudly.

"One what?" asked Shalan sleepily.

"Remember Danielle?"

"Danielle, who?"

"You know, that I talked to in 10th grade."

"Kind of. What about her?"

"She's dark-skinned."

"I know you didn't wake me up to tell me that. Bye." As she closed her eyes again, the phone rang. *Now what?*

"I promise not to call again, but a while ago you said you'd been kissed before. Who you been kissing, girl?"

"Good night, Levi." Shalan put the phone on the hook and turned over to sleep, a smile on her face.

Chapter 8

A few months later Shalan was sitting in Levi's backyard. They were having a bon voyage party for him. Although Shalan tried to feel festive, she felt as if she were at a wake. Levi was paying special attention to the girl he had taken to the prom; only today, she was poster girl for the perfect girlfriend for your son around Mr. and Mrs. Leach. Shalan felt an unfamiliar emotion pass through her. It felt almost like jealously. She shook it off as the DJ started playing the "Electric Slide." She jumped up and got in the line, and was soon enjoying herself. Later, after staying and helping clean up, she said goodnight to everyone.

"Wait, I'll walk you home," Levi told her. Her parents had left the party about an hour before it was over. When they reached her house, they stood in front of the steps not saying anything. "Well, I'm not going to call you in the morning before I leave, so I guess this is goodbye."

"What time are you pulling out?"

"Probably about 6:00, no later than 7. I'm going to miss you, you know."

"I'm going to miss you, too."

"I'm going to see if the folks can come up for Homecoming or something, if they can, you wanna come, too?"

"Is grits grocery?" She used one of Miss Frances' favorite phrases.

Levi smiled. "A'right, girl, you take care of yourself. Love you, girl." He gave her a brief hug and was gone.

As Shalan lay in bed that night, she replayed his words in her mind. Although she knew Levi meant he loved her as a sister, still the "love you, girl" had sounded good coming out of his mouth. "I love you, too, Levi," she whispered to her pillow. At 6:30 a.m. she stood on her porch and watched Levi back his car out of his yard and head for Washington, DC.

Chapter 9

Over the next couple of years, Shalan kept busy with her schoolwork and extra curricular activities. During her junior and senior years, her family and the Leaches went to Howard's homecomings. She, Hugh, and Angie went to the Cherry Blossom Festival in DC during her senior year. Levi came home for Thanksgiving, Christmas, and the occasional weekend. The summer after his freshman year was like old times.

Shalan got a shock Levi's sophomore year when he announced he was moving off campus to share an apartment with three other guys. Since they got a discount for signing a long-term lease, they were going to keep the apartment during the summer months. "I'll probably keep my part-time job over the summer and maybe take a class or two," was the way Levi logically explained it.

Does he always have to be so practical? Shalan wondered. She was seeing someone on a regular basis by Christmas of her senior year. Zac was from a neighboring county and was attending the local community college. She had seen him play basketball against her high school, but had never met him until he started attending CCCC. They met at the bowling alley one Saturday when she was hanging with some of her friends. He and some of his teammates were bowling in the next lane, and they began flirting with the girls. Before the afternoon was over, they had mixed up the two teams and phone numbers had been exchanged. Shalan accepted a movie date for the next weekend. Zac had wanted to go out the first night they met, but Shalan told him they needed to talk on the phone and get to know each other a little better before going out. She chuckled aloud the first time they rode down her street.

"What's funny?"

"Oh, nothing. I just thought about something, that's all."

"Care to share?"

"I have a good friend who lives in that house we just passed. He's away at college now and I was just thinking you're the first guy I've gone out with that he hasn't given the once over."

"Oh, sounds like y'all are *real* good friends."

"We are. Not the dating kind of friends, but the brother/sister kind of friends." "That's good to know, because I want to see a lot more of you."

"Oh, you do?"

"Yes, I sure do." Zac reached across the seat and gave her hand a squeeze. He gave her a significant look before turning his attention back to his driving.

Shalan went to all of Zac's home games and to some of his away games, too. She had talked to Levi about him on the phone, telling him how well he could play and how nice he was. Levi told her he couldn't wait to come home and see how much game he had. "Just tell him to meet me in the backyard at the goal, let me see what he can do."

"Why do you always have to be so competitive?"

"Oh, so now I'm competitive? Just 'cause I want to see if the brother got any skills?"

As it turned out, Levi and Zac never got to meet. Zac was playing in an all-star Christmas tournament. By the time he got home, Levi had returned to Washington.

Shalan had spent the morning of her senior prom at the beauty parlor and at the nail salon. Now she and Angie were experimenting with makeup. Angie was going to the prom, too, with a boy from church she had been dating since her sophomore year.

"Guess who's coming home?"

"I don't have to guess. Your brother."

"Yep."

"I knew he wasn't going to let you go to the prom without seeing you."

"He's probably coming to see you, too."

"We ought to put on a lot of makeup and let him think that's how we're going."

"No, don't give my brother a heart attack. He's probably going to be up worrying anyway until we get back." As they were giggling together, Shalan's phone rang.

"Hello."

"Hey, baby." It was Zac.

"Hey, what's up?" There was silence on the other end. "Zac? What's wrong?"

"Oh, man. Baby, I don't know how to tell you this."

Shalan knew that whatever it was, it wasn't going to be anything she wanted to hear. "Just tell me and get it over with. You're not taking me to the prom, are you?"

"No, I'm not. You know I told you about the girl I went with all through high school? Dee Dee?"

"Yeah, what about her?"

"She came to see me last week and we hooked back up."

"Let me get this straight," Shalan's voice was beginning to break she was so angry, "you got back together last week and you wait until the day of the prom to tell me you aren't going to take me!"

"I was still going to take you, but Dee Dee, well, she just wasn't having it. And that's what's up. I bet you gonna be lookin' all sweet and everything. Baby, you don't know how sorry I am."

"Yeah, you're sorry all right. About as sorry as they come." She slammed the phone down and tried to keep her voice from trembling when she turned back to Angie. "I guess you heard?"

"Yeah, that sorry dog! Wait up, maybe Levi can take you."

"No, his name has to be on the guest list."

"We could try."

"No, I'm just not going."

"Yes, you are. You can go with me and Mike."

"Thanks, Angie, but I wouldn't do that to you and Mike."

"Listen, girl, you are not staying home having a pity party. You're going with us because if it were the other way around you would do it for me. We'll pick you up at 7 so we can eat first."

"Just pick me up after you eat."

"No."

"Please?"

"Okay, we'll be here by 8:30."

At 6:30 the phone rang. It was Angie. "Hey, I know it's short notice, but can you be ready by 7:30? Something came up."

"Yeah, I'll start getting ready now." At 7:15 Shalan's mother declared her ready. George Sanders was in the living room trying to pick out the best spot to take pictures. Nancy tried to prepare him for how beautiful and grown up their daughter looked, but he had to see for himself. The love and pride in his eyes made Shalan feel special despite being stood up on such a special day in her life."

"You look beautiful, baby. If you look like this for the prom, I can't imagine how you'll look on your wedding day. Just don't let it be anytime soon." He gave her a hug, being careful not to wrinkle her gown.

"Thank you, Daddy." They took several shots of her alone and some with each of her parents. At 7:30 sharp the doorbell rang.

"Come in," George called. He had gotten out the video camera. Shalan looked up expecting to see Mike and Angie. Instead she saw Levi dressed in a black tuxedo with a red bow tie and a matching cumber band, holding a corsage.

"What are you doing here?" Shalan asked.

"Coming to take my best friend to her senior prom. Close your mouth, it takes away from the overall effect."

"But you have to be on the guest list. You know that."

"Detail, my dear, mere detail." He pinned the corsage on her. "On the serious tip, you look good, girl." He gave her his special wink. "I had a feeling you'd be the lady in red tonight... Hungry?" Levi inquired once they had gotten in his dad's car.

"No, I ate already because I didn't want to be the third wheel with Angie and Mike."

"Okay, maybe we'll get something afterward. Hey, I'm sorry about Zac and everything, but I'm glad I'm getting to take you to your prom. Are you okay with all of this?"

"Yeah, it's all good. Zac just better not call me anymore."

"I heard that. Anyway, forget that clown, because tonight we're going to get our party on."

The night was magical for Shalan. She had a much better time than she would have had with Zac. In spite of all the years she and Levi had known one another and danced together, they had never danced close before. It felt a little strange at first, but by the second time, they fit in each other's arms comfortably. Shalan worried that he could hear her heart beating through her dress. She shouldn't be reacting this way about her best friend, should she? *Maybe it's just the atmosphere*, she reasoned. She forced herself to take a deep breath and relax.

"You okay, hon?"

Hon? Was that hon as in honey, you're special, or hon as in you're like a sister to me? "Yeah, I'm straight."

Later, as they drove home, Shalan couldn't think of a thing to say. *Why am I tripping like this? This is good ol' Levi!* But she had to admit good ol' Levi looked better than she'd ever seen him look. Maybe it was because she didn't see him that often that she was suddenly aware of his good looks.

"So did you have a good time?"

"Yes," she answered. Then more softly, almost shyly, she added, "Thanks for taking me and thanks for not making a lot of comments about Zac standing me up."

"I was glad to. And about your boy? You don't need me to tell you anything about him, do you? You know what's up with him. You deserve better than him, just remember that, okay?"

"Okay."

"I'm heading back as soon as I get a few hours sleep, but I'll call you later in the week." He walked her to the door and gave her a kiss on the forehead. "See ya."

It was a long time before Shalan closed her eyes that early morning.

Chapter 10

Over the next couple of years, Shalan was a student herself. She had decided to go to North Carolina Central University in Durham. She adapted quickly to campus life, joining the gospel choir and the newspaper staff. Some weekends she took two or three of her new friends, who lived out of state, home with her. Other weekends they stayed on campus to attend the games. A time or two she went home with friends. She and Levi didn't see each other as much, but managed to keep in touch through email and the occasional letter or card. The shock of Levi staying in DC year round was nothing compared to the news Angie called to give her during her sophomore year. The Leach family was moving from the old neighborhood. They were buying a bigger house in the outskirts of Sanford. Levi, Hugh and Angie were all in college by this time. Hugh was at NC State in Raleigh, and Angie was a freshman at A&T University in Greensboro. Greg, Rod, and Pamela were still in school. Angie and Shalan both felt like they were moving 100 miles away. Even though college had separated them, this felt like a major change in their lives.

I'm going to miss you, girl."

"I'm going to miss you, too. You gotta come see us, though."

"I will and don't forget to come back and see me."

"It'll feel funny passing by our house seeing someone else living there. I've never lived anywhere else."

"Yeah, I feel you."

The summer after the Leaches moved, Shalan was home alone for a few days. Her parents and another couple had gone to Florida. They had been planning the trip for months. Shalan had to keep reassuring them that she was an adult and could take care of herself. She couldn't help wishing that Angie, Hugh, and especially Levi were still in the neighborhood. Later, while sitting on the porch, she saw Levi drive up. It was as if she had conjured him up. She ran down the steps and gave him a big hug. This was the first time she had seen him since he graduated from Howard.

"Girl, look at you. You picked up a little weight, didn't you? It looks good on you."

"Thanks. Look, I'm sorry I didn't make it to your graduation."

"Don't worry about that. I understood. So how've you been?"

"Good. How about you?"

"I've been good, too. I came by to tell you Pamela won the oratorical contest."

"Good for her! I'll have to call her." They both went and sat on the porch swing. Levi acted as though something else was on his mind. He kept looking in her eyes. When she looked away and glanced back, he was still staring. "What?" she finally asked him.

"Can I ask you something without you getting offended?"

"Since when did you start worrying about offending me?"

"I'm serious."

"Okay, ask me."

Levi stretched and blew a breath out. "Have you ever thought about me as more than a friend? Be honest."

"What do you mean?" Shalan thought she understood the question, but she didn't want to make a fool of herself.

"Baby, don't. We're more than that. Don't act like you don't know what I'm asking."

"Okay, once or twice I kind of wondered what it would be like to be more than friends." *Once or twice? Yeah, right.*

"For real?"

"For real."

He leaned over and kissed her gently, then more passionately. "Oh, Shalan. You're so sweet." He held her tighter as their kisses grew deeper and deeper. Shalan gave a soft moan. "Do you want me to stop?" he asked.

"No."

"Can we go inside? Shalan, I want to make love to you, honey."

"You do?" Shalan asked huskily.

"Yes, very much." She stood and reached for his hand. When they reached her bedroom, Levi closed and locked the door even though her parents were miles away. He sat in the chair beside her bed and called her to him. Holding her on his lap, he kissed her again. "Oh, honey. I've been wanting to do this since I took you to the prom."

"You have?" In the back of her mind Shalan was wondering where her ability to make more than two word sentences had gone.

"Yes. Tell me to stop, because, baby, I can't."

"I don't want you to stop."

He led her gently to the bed and made love to her. Afterward they both fell asleep. Shalan woke up to see Levi standing by the window looking dejectedly out. "What's wrong?" He faced her and she saw that he had tears in his eyes.

"First of all, let me say how sorry I am for what just happened. No, don't look at me like I'm saying I didn't want you because I did. I wanted you more than I've ever wanted anyone, but the timing is wrong. Some heavy stuff is going on in my life, Shalan. I wanted to come by and tell you what direction my life is going in."

"I'm listening."

"I... You know I got saved last year, right?"

"Yeah, but I never understood that. We've always been in the church."

"Yeah, Shalan, we've always been in the church, but the church hasn't always been in us. There's a difference, a big difference. When you get saved, it's like Jesus is a personal friend. And I wish everyone I know could experience this same joy. I can't describe it."

"So is that what you wanted to talk to me about?"

"Yeah, that, too, but there are some other things. I'm going in the ministry. I'm moving to Atlanta to attend the seminary."

"Hold up, you're going to be a preacher? When did you decide this?"

"I didn't decide. I have a calling on my life. This is what God's calling me to do, and I've got to be obedient. When you give your life to Jesus, you do everything you can to stay in His will. And what I just did, well I know God is not pleased with that."

"You're talking about what we just did?"

"Yeah."

"Sex is only wrong if you're cheating on your husband or wife, committing adultery, so why would God get mad or even care if we wanted to make love?"

"Because sex is for marriage and..." The telephone ringing interrupted what Levi was about to say. It was Angie.

"Is Levi over there?"

"Yeah, he's here." Shalan smiled thinking of how shocked Angie would be when she found out she and Levi were "talking."

"Tell him I wish he would come home so his girlfriend can stop calling every 10 minutes."

"His girlfriend?" asked Shalan deadpan.

"Yeah, some Miss Thang named Ariana or something like that. We met her at graduation."

"Oh, did she have the usual tall, light-skinned, high maintenance look?" Levi looked up at her.

"You know him, don't you?"

"Uh-huh. I'll tell him." Shalan's throat felt like it was closing up, but she refused to show any emotion as she relayed Angie's message to Levi. "So tell God not to worry about me anymore. It's Ariana He has to worry about you lusting after."

"Shalan, come here. Look at me." Levi reached for her.

"No, I just want you to go."

"Ariana is not my girlfriend."

"Oh, so how did she get your home number?"

"She met Momma and Dad at graduation. I guess she remembered his name and called 411. I didn't give it to her. Do you think I would have made love to you just now if I were involved with someone?"

"Levi, you must have forgotten who you're talking to. I know you don't have a problem with seeing two women at the same time."

"I'm not like that anymore, baby, you've got to believe me."

"I don't know what to believe. First you get me in the bed. Then you tell me, 'Oops, my bad, I didn't mean to do that. I just wanted to talk about the Lord.' Just go, okay?"

"Shalan, please, can't we sit down and talk?"

"What part of go don't you understand? At least Zac didn't try to lie and say he was a Christian."

A hurt look came on Levi's face. "I'll go. Just call me later when you've had time to cool off. I have some serious things I need to talk to you about. Okay?"

Shalan turned her back to him. Levi put his hands on her shoulders and tried to turn her around. "Leave me alone, Levi. I'm not playing." Levi let himself out of the house.

Chapter 11

The phone rang persistently all day, but Shalan refused to answer it. Around 11 that night she heard someone knocking at the door. *He just doesn't get it,* she thought. Then she heard a woman's voice calling her name. It sounded like Miss Frances from next door. She peeped out and saw Miss Frances and a policeman. *Oh, my God. Levi must have told Miss Frances I won't answer the phone and she's called the police.*

"Just a minute." Shalan pulled her robe on and went to answer the door. Miss Frances was crying. "I'm okay, Miss Frances, I just didn't feel like answering the phone."

"Sit down, baby," said Miss Frances.

"Are you alone?" asked the policeman.

"Yes, why, what's wrong?"

"There's been an accident, baby. Nancy and George are both gone," Miss Frances told her.

"Gone?"

"I'm sorry to tell you this, but your parents are both dead," the policeman told her as gently as possible.

"Not my mama and daddy! NO! NO! NO!"

Miss Frances held her as they both sobbed. "I'm staying here with you tonight. Do you want me to call the Leaches?"

"No. I need to call my Aunt Faye in New York and my Uncle Chip in South Carolina. I'll call the Leaches tomorr…" Before she could finish the sentence, a fresh wave of grief hit her. "Call Angie. Tell her to please come."

Chapter 12

Shalan closed the house up after the double funeral and went to New York to spend a few weeks with her Aunt Faye. Her aunt told her to stay as long as she wanted to, even telling her she could stay and finish college up there. Faye, her mother's sister, was divorced with a daughter six months older than Shalan. The cousins got along well, but didn't see each other too often. LaTia, her cousin, wanted to pursue a modeling career and was constantly updating her portfolio and looking for that one lucky break. Since both young women favored their mothers, they looked a lot alike. LaTia, however was 5'10", and Shalan was barely 5 feet. The other difference was that Shalan was unaware of how pretty she was. LaTia was always telling her to have confidence in herself.

Shalan decided to take the fall semester off. She thought about finding a job to keep from losing her mind, but she couldn't face books and tests right now. She had talked to Angie several times on the phone, and although she had accepted Levi's sympathy, she refused his attempts to have any kind of personal conversation. Levi had already left for Atlanta the last time she talked to Angie. Six weeks after her parents' deaths, she went home. She had decided to keep the house, but she didn't want to live in it right now. There were too many memories. She was going to put most of the furniture in storage, taking only her bedroom suit and the den furniture, and moving to a one- bedroom apartment. As she sorted her parents' things, a wave of nausea hit her. She went to the kitchen and fixed herself a glass of coke. She hadn't been feeling well lately. She had thought it was from all of the stress she had been under lately, but now, as she thought about it, she considered the possibility that she might be pregnant. *Oh, my God, please, not that, not now.* She picked up the phone to call Angie, but slowly replaced the receiver. She couldn't confide in Angie and risk having her tell Levi. Anyway, suppose it was a false alarm, then Angie and probably Hugh and the whole family would know she and Levi had "done it." But she didn't want to face this alone. She looked in her purse and dug out her cell phone. Maybe LaTia could tell her what to do.

"Hello."

"LaTia, girl, I'm glad you have your phone on. Are you home?"

"No, why?"

"I didn't want you to say anything, Aunt Faye might overhear."

"All right, girl, what's going on? Are you in North Carolina?"

"Yeah, I'm home." Then before she lost her nerve she blurted out, "Tia, I think I might be pregnant."

"Whoa, I didn't even know you had a man."

"I don't have a man, it's just…"

"Then it must be Levi's."

"Now why would you say that?" So much for keeping the father's name a secret.

"Girl, Stevie Wonder can see how you feel about that man! Shoot, if I hadn't seen the way you looked at him, I would have cracked on him myself. Brother knows he fine."

"It's not like that. We're just friends."

"Uh huh. So, it's not his baby?"

"I don't even know if there *is* a baby, Tia."

"Okay, just slow your roll. First we need to find out for sure."

"Tia, can I trust you? I'm going crazy."

"You know you can trust me. You know enough of my secrets, don't you? Okay, this is what I'm going to do. I'm about to call Tyrese and see if he can bring me down there. Get one of those home pregnancy kits, but don't use it until I get there."

"You don't have to come all the way down here. I just needed someone to talk to, that's all."

"No, I don't like the way you sound. Besides I've got to check on my future godchild. I am the godmother, aren't I?"

"Sure, if there's a baby, you can be the godmother. Thanks, Tia, I love you."

"I love you, too. Hang in there. I'll be there as soon as I can."

"What are you going to tell your mother?"

"Just that you need help closing the house up and that you've decided to come to New York after all."

"Yes, I guess I will be going back with you. Oh, and Tia, it *is* Levi's baby."

"I know. See you later."

Chapter 13

After hanging up, Shalan wandered over to the window and looked out. An overwhelming sadness came over her. Aunt Faye hadn't wanted her to come alone, but she didn't have any vacation time left. She had wanted her to wait until the first long weekend before she sorted through her parents' things so she wouldn't have to face it by herself. But she had felt the need to go ahead and do what needed to be done. Not even calling Angie or Hugh, she had flown into RDU and had her former roommate drive her to Sanford. She placed her hand on her flat stomach and wondered how she would manage with a baby on her own. EPT or not, she felt certain she was pregnant. Telling Levi was not an option. What kind of minister had illegitimate children? And knowing his family, they might convince him to marry her. What kind of marriage would that be with him in love with someone else? Even if he wasn't in love with someone else, Shalan knew she wasn't his type in the looks department.

She thought about her mama and daddy as tears rolled down her face. Would they have been disappointed in her, she wondered. Knowing her folks, they would have made the best of the situation and welcomed their first grandchild into their home with open arms and loving hearts. There would have been no keeping it a secret from the Leaches if her folks were alive. She didn't really want to live in New York, but she couldn't very well stay here and keep it a secret. But then again, she couldn't very well ask Aunt Faye to take her and a baby in. Maybe she could find her own place in New York, or maybe she could pay Aunt Faye rent until the baby came, then find a place of her own. She was the sole beneficiary of her parents' life insurance policies, so if she didn't get foolish, she could manage for a while.

After a lot of soul searching, Shalan once again turned to the task of packing up a house full of memories. She decided to donate all of her parents' clothing to the church's clothes closet. Should she rent the house completely furnished since she wasn't moving to an apartment? Or should she put everything in storage? There were some pieces she knew she wanted to keep, but was it worth it to pay a storage fee for a long period of time? *Oh, I don't know what to do*, she lamented. With that, she went to the room she had grown up in and curled up on her bed. Shalan never knew when the sun set, because she cried herself to sleep.

At 2:00 the next morning, the ringing phone jarred her from a deep sleep. "Hello?" she answered groggily.

"Hey, it's us. We're in your driveway; come open the door."

"Okay."

"You don't have a problem with Tyrese staying here, do you?"

"Girl, please." She hung up and went to answer the door.

"Hey, Tyrese. Thanks for bringing Tia."

"Hi, no problem."

"I know you're tired so I'll show you the guest room."

"Okay, and can I grab a quick shower?"

"Sure, I'll show you where everything is. Just make yourself at home."

After she came back in the living room, Tia asked, "Did you get the you know what?"

"No, I didn't go anywhere after I talked to you."

"That's all right. I stopped and bought two."

"Come on, let's go in Mama and Daddy's room." The first test came back positive. They decided to get some sleep and take a second test the first thing in the morning. LaTia fell asleep quickly, but Shalan, having rested earlier, saw the dawn of a new day.

Chapter 14

Early the next morning, Shalan tiptoed to the master bathroom and took the second pregnancy test. Before the results were in she knew without confirmation that she was indeed carrying Levi's baby beneath her heart. She had mixed feelings about bringing life into the world. Surely her life would never be the same again. After the loss of her parents, it seemed almost comforting to know she would have immediate family again in less than a year. For a fleeting moment she thought about phoning Levi, and just as quickly dismissed the notion. Levi was going to be a minister, a man of God! she reminded herself. Knowing Levi, he would offer to marry her, but baby or no baby, she absolutely refused to marry a man who was in love with someone else. She rubbed her stomach. *It will be you and me, baby. Mama promises to love you always. If it's a boy, I'll give him part of Dad's name, and if it's a girl, I'll name her after Mom.* By the time LaTia got out of bed, Shalan had resigned herself to being a single mom in New York City.

The three of them got a lot done that day and the next. With a last look at the house she had grown up in, Shalan climbed in the car to head back north. She had said her goodbyes to Miss Frances the night before, but had not contacted anyone else.

As it turned out, shortly after they returned to New York, Aunt Faye had to get an unlisted phone number to keep an unwanted fan of Tia's from calling. By changing her cell phone number, Shalan was able to sever all ties with the Leaches. It hurt to imagine how Angie and the rest of the family probably worried about her, but she felt she had no choice. She promised herself that she would contact Angie when the baby was older. Her son, Kendrick George Sanders arrived on February 17th, one month early, but in perfect health. She had started taking business classes before he was born, and continued at night after he was born. Shalan and little Kendrick stayed with her Aunt Faye until he was six months old before moving to an apartment with Tia. Tia's modeling career had really taken off, and she was now supporting herself strictly from modeling jobs. "You know, Shalan, I could probably get you some jobs."

"Thanks, but no thanks. One diva in the family is enough." Shalan had a well paying job as an administrative assistant to the CEO of a large hospital. One day when Kendrick had just turned three, Tia came in, squealing. She and Tyrese had been on a cruise to Jamaica.

"Guess what?"

"Umm, let me see." Shalan pretended to think hard. "Judging by the rock on your finger I would say you got engaged."

"Yes, and, girl, you've got to help me get it together. He wants to get married in June, and here it is already March!"

"We can do it. We just need to get started."

"Thanks, Shalan. You know I want you to be my maid of honor, and Kendrick my ring bearer."

"Okay, sure." Eagerly the girls made plans. Tyrese's daughter from a previous relationship would be the flower girl. Tia decided on having just two other attendants and letting her other friends serve as hostesses at the reception. Tyrese would have a best man and two groomsmen and use his other friends as ushers.

"Before we get too carried away, we'd better call Aunt Faye and tell her the news."

"Yeah, you're right. Oh, Shalan, girl, I am so happy! And one day when it's your turn, I'll be your matron of honor."

"Don't hold your breath on that one."

"Listen to me, your day *is* coming. And you are going to make a beautiful bride. I don't know who has you thinking you're not pretty, but girl you are beautiful on the outside and the inside. The only reason you don't have a man is because you don't want one. Now come on, we've got to go over to Mom's."

Chapter 15

LaTia's wedding turned out beautifully. It was held in her church, with the reception following in a hotel ballroom. Shalan felt a twinge of sadness as LaTia and Tyrese danced their first dance as man and wife. Would she ever fall in love? Or to put it more accurately, would she ever fall out of love so that she could fall in love again? Being Tia's maid of honor was not the biggest thing to happen to Shalan that year. In April she had accepted Jesus as her personal Savior. Now she understood what Levi had been trying to tell her all those years ago. It felt so good to have a personal relationship with Jesus. She had been attending Bible study faithfully since April.

Now that Tia was a married woman, Shalan would be moving out of the apartment the next week while the newlyweds were on their honeymoon. Although Tia was moving to Tyrese's place, Shalan had made a decision to leave New York. At first she considered returning to North Carolina, settling in another city, but for some reason had decided to move to Maryland. Just last week, she had purchased a Ford Explorer, and she and Kendrick would be driving to Maryland. Since one of her college friends was from Baltimore, she decided to look at some cities near there. She and Kendrick could stay in a motel for a few weeks while she looked for a job and a place to stay. Common sense told her to look for a job before moving, but something else was telling her to move now. Could it be the leading of the Holy Spirit?

Chapter 16

The Present

Shalan slept late the morning after the revival. She had talked late into the night, sharing highlights of her life growing up on the same street with Levi. When she came downstairs, Kendrick was dressed and eating a bowl of cereal. "I overslept, too," Mother Ingram told her. "I was just about to send Kendrick up to get you. When I got up, he was watching *The Wiggles.* As soon as he saw me, he wanted to know when breakfast would be ready."

"If I hurry, I won't be too late. Let me call and tell them I'm on the way."

"I already called, grab a piece of toast or something before you go. I'm going to drop Kendrick off for you."

"Oh, thank you, Mother Ingram. I appreciate everything you do for us, and thanks for listening last night."

"Honey, you know you're welcome. I've been wondering what to tell Perry. I know he's going to want to know what happened."

"I know. I don't want him to think hard of Levi and keep him from getting the job."

"Perry is not that narrow-minded. But he won't put you in an uncomfortable position either. You won't leave us if Levi becomes pastor, will you?"

"No, but I'm not sure about staying at the church. It would depend on Levi."

"Perry would have to give a reason for not wanting Levi, and I don't know how you want to handle that."

"Well, right now, I'm just going to go to work and not worry about it. Besides, little pitchers have big ears," she said, glancing at Kendrick.

Chapter 17

Levi hadn't fared much better during the night. The Lamars had ambushed him on his way to his room. Vanessa was a beautiful girl, but there was something about her that grated on his nerves. She had followed him into his room instead of going on to the suite with her parents. All he had wanted to do was lie back and think about Shalan. That had been the shock of the century seeing Shalan. How was that for coincidence, her being a member of the church where he was running a revival! Talk about pretty! She had looked so pretty in that purple dress. Purple had always been his favorite color, but he couldn't remember ever seeing Shalan dressed in purple. Her favorite color had always been red, and that's what she wore on special occasions. She always thought he preferred tall, light-skinned women, but in reality, he had always thought Shalan was the most attractive girl he knew. He had treasured her friendship so much that he had been afraid to take it to another level. Then when he did, he had blown it. Shalan had dropped off the face of the earth. He had made love to her and never even told her he loved her. Now she had a son. He felt a stab of jealousy. Had she been wearing a ring? He hadn't noticed; he was too busy making a fool out of himself. Brother Ingram had mentioned that she was living with his mother. He needed to find out how to get in touch with her and apologize. Maybe he would just wait and see if she showed up at church tonight. Then he hit himself on the forehead, remembering that he would be chaperoned by Vanessa and her parents.

As if on cue, the telephone rang. Thinking it was Vanessa, but hoping it wasn't, Levi reached for the phone. "Hello?"

"Hi, darling."

"Hi, Vanessa. How are you this morning?"

"Fine. We're about to go grab some breakfast. Why don't you

come down?"

"You all go ahead. I don't want to eat anything right now."

"Well at least come sit with us and drink some coffee. What will my parents think if we came all this way to see you and you ignore us? When I tried to talk to you last night you acted like your mind was a million miles away."

With a sigh, Levi agreed to come down in a few minutes. *First of all,* he grumbled to himself, *you could tell your parents to wait for an invitation before barging in. Secondly you could tell them that maybe, just maybe, I want to spend some quality time with the Lord before tonight.*

Or, the Devil put in, *she could tell them you want to daydream about Shalan.*

I know one thing, Levi thought, *I need to start this day with prayer*. He put the *Do Not Disturb* sign on the door and knelt in prayer. He was feeling considerably better when he finally joined the Lamars, offering to take them sightseeing.

Chapter 18

Tonight was the last night of revival. Levi had managed to get a few hours of solitude before coming to the church. He dreaded facing Perry Ingram because he had really come to like and look up to the older man this week. He could only imagine what he must be thinking of him now. His fears went unfounded, however. Perry greeted him as cheerfully as ever. Both men started apologizing at the same time. "I just want to say I'm sorry about the way I spoke to Shalan last night. And like I told you, I will apologize to her. Is she coming tonight?"

"I'm not sure. I want to apologize, too. I shouldn't have said what I did about your girlfriend. I'm sure she's a nice young woman or you wouldn't be interested in her. Also, I shouldn't have interrupted you while you were meditating. How are you feeling tonight?"

"Good, Brother Ingram, I'm feeling good."

"Glad to hear it. Well, I'll leave you alone now. Talk to you later."

"All right."

Levi walked down the hall from the study on his way to the sanctuary. He felt especially energized and anointed. Right before he entered the sanctuary, he heard Shalan giving a moving testimony. *So Shalan is saved now*, he thought. *Praise the Lord*! *Maybe that will make her more open to an apology from me*. On the less selfish side, Levi was just glad within his heart that someone so dear to him had accepted Jesus. He would have to tell his mother. *His mother!* He hadn't even had time today to call her and tell her Shalan was living here! They had often wondered what had become of Shalan after she moved to New York.

As the praise team took their seats, he walked to the pulpit. One of the deacons stood up to introduce him, telling the waiting congregation that if they had not yet heard him, they were in for a treat. He told those who had been there all week that he knew they were waiting anxiously, just as he was, to see what word the Lord would give them tonight. "After two selections from the Gospel Choir, the next voice you hear will be the man of God, Rev. Levi Leach." When the choir came up front, Levi was pleasantly surprised to see that Shalan was among them. She led "Now Behold the Lamb" in her sweet soprano voice. The choir was actually good, Levi thought. There were 10 of them—four altos, three sopranos, and three men. One of the men played the keyboards. As they finished the song, one of the women said they had a request to sing "My Soul Has Been Anchored in the Lord" but they were not going to be able to do it because the leader was hoarse. There were audible groans from the congregation. Before he thought about what he was doing, Levi stood up.

"It seems like that song is a favorite, and if it's going to bless somebody's soul, I'll sing it for you tonight. If I can get this wonderful choir to back me up. It's been a long time since I heard this song, so y'all just bear with me if I forget the words and help me out." There were Amens and applause. The keyboard player went into the musical introduction. Then with his eyes closed, trying to hear Douglas Miller's voice in his head, Levi began to sing in his gifted voice… *"Though the storms keep on raging in my life and sometimes it's hard to tell the night from the day, still that hope that lies within is reassured as I keep my eyes toward the distant shore…"*

Before he finished singing, the congregation was on its feet. Many were crying and praising the Lord. Shalan was so full of the spirit she was barely able to finish the song.

It didn't matter because the congregation was singing the background along with the choir. Vanessa and her parents came in about midway through the song. They had never heard Levi sing. "Why is he singing with the choir?" Vanessa whispered to her dad.

"I came in with you, remember? All I know is that it's a good thing this is his last night here. These people have him brainwashed."

"Shh," Mrs. Lamar told her husband and daughter. They settled back to see what would happen next. Levi went back to the pulpit.

"How many of you are anchored in the Lord tonight? When you're anchored in the Lord, I declare unto you, the billows can roar, the dashers can break, but God has it all under control. Don't you feel sometimes that the storms of life toss you around like a piece of paper? But isn't it good to have that assurance—that blessed assurance that your soul is anchored in the Lord? Oh, I don't know about you, but I feel good tonight. If I don't say another word, the Lord has truly blessed me. God is moving by His spirit. I feel the presence of God in such a mighty way right now that I'm going to ask that person or persons who came here tonight searching for something to come to the altar right now. The Spirit is telling me that if I start preaching right now the Devil is going to talk someone out of what they need. I don't know who it is, but someone came here tonight. Hallelujah, thank you, Holy Spirit. It's a young woman. She wants to give up on life, but she came by the church just to see if God had a word. You see, she grew up in the church, but somewhere along the way she turned away from everything that her parents taught her. And now she thinks death is the answer, but I came to declare unto you tonight that the Devil is a liar. If you're not too embarrassed to come up here, I want to pray with you. If you don't want to come now, please don't leave this service without seeing me. This is not a show, church. I came here tonight prepared to go another way, but the Spirit is telling me otherwise. Everyone, bow your heads and begin to intercede." As the church prayed, a young woman who looked to be about 20 began to wail. Levi looked up with tears running down his face. "Thank you, Jesus. Thank you, Lord. Will one of the mothers of the church bring her to me?"

Mother Ingram went and embraced the girl and together they made their way to the front of the church. Levi took her hands in both of his. He looked at her for minutes before he spoke. "You're just passing through. You've been running from a situation where you thought you might lose your life if you didn't run. But now you're tired of running and the Devil has told you to take your own life, that way no one else can take it. I don't know all the details, I don't need to know, but you passed by this church. And you wanted to come in just for a little while to see if God still loves you. Yes, the Lord is saying He loves you and He wants you to stop running—stop running from the people that threatened you, and stop running from Him. Just to let you know how much the Lord loves you, I have never in my ministry done what I'm doing now. But God wanted you so badly that He has taken me to another level tonight just for this moment. Will you let me pray for you?" The girl nodded.

"Father God, I don't know this young lady, I don't know what or who has made her want to give up on life. But, Lord, You know all things. Lord, You made her, You know all about her. Lord, I know it was no accident that she happened upon this church at this appointed time. Lord, speak to her right now. Let her feel Your love once again, because it's been a while, Lord, since she felt love. God, give her direction and guidance. Lord, let her know that nothing's too hard for you. In Jesus' name, we pray. We count it done. Amen."

The young woman continued to weep. "I want some of the women of the church to just come make a circle around this young girl. Let her feel your warmth and your love. Someone else has been in a situation before where they didn't know which way to turn."

After a few minutes the girl asked to have words.

"My name is Sheba. I just turned 20 last week, and I haven't seen my family in four years. My father pastors a church in South Carolina and I got tired of going to church and being the preacher's daughter. I met this guy and left town with him. We ended up in Philly and he joined a gang." Her voice started trembling, but she fought for control and continued. "After awhile I wanted to go home, but he told me he would kill me. He said he could make a phone call and have my whole family killed. Last week he got arrested and, while he was in jail, I started hitchhiking home. I had some money, but it got stolen at the rest stop I was sleeping in. I started to call my folks, but then I got scared that I might get them killed. They probably think I'm dead, so I decided maybe it would be better for everyone if I were dead. Then I was walking by here and heard the singing, and I… I."

"That's okay, darling," said Mother Ingram as she embraced her. "Everything's going to be all right."

Chapter 19

After church dismissed, Levi made a call to Rev. Hampton in South Carolina. He told him briefly what Sheba had told the church. "Right now she's gone home with one of the mothers of the church, Mrs. Ingram, but she's going to call you once she's had something to eat."

"We're going to get in the car right now," said Rev. Hampton. "Give her my cell phone number. Tell my baby girl that we're coming to get her. And thank you, Pastor, thank you so much."

"I'm just glad I was here and able to help. Let me give you my cell phone number. When you get here just call me, and I'll take you to Mrs. Ingram's house."

"Okay, goodnight and God bless you."

"God bless you, too, sir." Levi had picked up the phone to call Sheba with the news when there was a loud knock on the study. "Just a minute," he called. Vanessa came on in.

"Are you ever going to be ready to leave?"

"Why don't you go on with your folks, I have a few things here to tie up."

"Hello, earth to Levi, you are not the pastor of this church. You are not even a member. Get your check and say goodbye. Let's go!"

"Vanessa, have your parents left yet?"

"No, why?"

"Because I would strongly suggest that you go find them and go back to the motel. I will talk to you later. I have a few things to tie up here." Vanessa could tell by the quiet way he said it that he was very angry. She decided to change tactics. She went over and kissed him on the cheek.

"Okay, love, just call me when you get in."

Perry stuck his head in the door. "Oh sorry, I thought you were alone in here. How are you?" he asked Vanessa.

"Fine," answered Vanessa. "I was just leaving." After she was gone, Perry asked Levi if he wanted to follow him to his mother's house.

"Well I was about to call, but do you think it would be okay?"

"Sure, I doubt if anyone's going to do much sleeping for a while."

"Okay, I want to see where she lives anyway so I can talk to Shalan."

Perry led Levi to the den where the three women were having a snack. Kendrick had been taken up to bed. Levi told Sheba what her father had said and gave her his phone number. "I'm going to make a call to Philly and see if I can find out if there's anything that can be done about the threats. I don't want you living in fear."

"Thank you. Everyone has been so nice."

"Hey, that's the way we do it. How are you, Mother Ingram?"

"I'm blessed. That was something the way the Lord used you tonight."

"Yes, ma'am, it was. Every time I think I know the Lord, He shows me another side of Himself."

"Child, I'll soon be knocking on 80's door and I still don't know everything there is to know about the Lord."

"I know that's right. How are you, Shalan?"

"I'm fine, and you?"

"Can't complain. Where's your little man? Sleep?"

"Yeah, I just took him up a few minutes ago."

Mother Ingram asked Levi would he like something to eat or drink. He eyed the chocolate cake and asked for a piece. Shalan started to the kitchen to get him a piece and something to drink. After she had left the room, Perry motioned for him to follow her.

"To your left and make a left," he said. Levi glanced over at Mother Ingram.

"What are you waiting for?" she asked. "I'm going to show Sheba where she can lie down and get some rest and also make her phone call. Then this old woman is going to call it a night."

"I'm going, too, Mama. Travis and I'll be over tomorrow to work in your yard, though."

"Okay, baby. Good night."

Shalan had started out of the kitchen when Levi walked in. Levi took the plate and glass from her and walked over to the table. "Will you sit with me for a minute? Please?"

"I need to get back to Sheba."

"Mother Ingram took her to the guest room to rest and to call her folks. Sit down for a minute, Shalan. I won't keep you long, I promise." Shalan reluctantly sat down just as Levi's cell phone rang. He glanced at the caller ID and saw that it was Vanessa's cell phone number. This was one time she was going to have to wait.

"Aren't you going to answer that?"

"As a matter of fact, I'm not. A ringing telephone caused a lot of misunderstanding between us before." Shalan felt her face color as she thought about the one time they had made love. "Girl, where have you been?"

"New York, here."

Levi just looked at her and shook his head. "First of all I want to say how sorry I am for the way I acted. Hey, I was way out of line and I'm so sorry."

"Don't worry about it."

He reached across the table and covered her hand. "I do worry about it. We go too far back for us to have anything negative to come between us."

"I accept your apology and it's good to see you again."

"Can I have a hug?" He came around the table, not waiting for an answer. Shalan stood up and gave him a hug. Levi squeezed her hard. "It is so good to see you. You look good. I like the way you're wearing your hair now."

"Yeah?"

"Yeah." Though Shalan had always had long hair that came below her shoulders, she used to wear it up in a French roll or a French braid. Now she was wearing it down with just a hint of curl to it.

"Oh, I saw your fiancée at church. She's pretty."

Levi gave a little laugh. "Actually she's not my fiancée."

Shalan gave a little laugh of her own. "Like Ariana wasn't your girlfriend?"

"Vanessa is my girlfriend, but I haven't proposed to her and I doubt that I will. *But* I wasn't lying to you that day when I said Ariana wasn't my girlfriend. If my sister hadn't called when she did, I was going to talk to you about *you* being my girlfriend. I just let my hormones get out of control. I was going to ask you if you had thought about accepting the Lord."

"Oh."

"That's all you can say, oh?"

"What am I supposed to say? It's water under the bridge now."

"So what about you? Is there a man in your life?"

"No, not right now." *No, not since you.*

"Is your son's father some dude you met in New York?"

"No."

"Okay, I won't pry, I can see you don't want to talk about it. I'll be leaving Sunday, but can we keep in touch?"

"Sure, let me give you my email address." She went to get paper and pen out of the kitchen drawer. Tearing it in half she wrote his on one piece and hers on the other.

"Momma and Angie are going to have a fit when I tell them I ran into you."

"How are they doing?"

"Doing fine. As a matter of fact, Angie's getting married New Year's Eve."

"Get out!"

"Yep."

"Is she marrying Mike?"

"Nah. She's marrying this brother she met at T."

"I guess I'll have to go home for that."

"Yeah, you will." Shalan was confused by the way he was looking at her and decided to change the subject.

"So are you going to become our pastor, or no?"

"Well, if I get an offer I'm definitely interested. I have to preach at this other church up here Sunday, but I don't think there's any possibility of me going there."

"Really?"

"Yeah, after tonight, I know I've got to go where I can be free, you know?"

"Uh huh. That was something. Has that happened to you before?"

"Never. But tonight it was like the Holy Spirit was whispering in my ear. I didn't even get to preach, but it was like it didn't matter. I did what I had to do."

"Yeah. I hope that guy doesn't come after her once he gets out of jail."

"I have a frat brother whose father is a detective in Philly. I'm going to call him tomorrow, but you know what, Shalan? I don't think the Lord would have sent her to us for us to intervene on His behalf if He were going to let her die anyway. I believe that. I think Sheba is going to be all right."

"I do, too. We'll just have to keep her lifted up in prayer."

"Oh, I heard your testimony tonight. I'm so glad you got saved."

"Me, too. It has really changed my life."

"Look, I'm not going to sit here and talk all night. I'm going to let you get some rest. Is it okay if I give Angie your phone number?"

"Yeah, that's fine."

"Okay, well I'm going to get out of here. I'll probably call you tomorrow, okay?"

"Okay. I'll walk you to the door."

When they got to the door, Levi stood there as if he were reluctant to leave. Finally, with a peck on her cheek, he told her good night.

Chapter 20

Levi alternated between reading his Bible and gazing out of the window Saturday night. The day had been equally rewarding and depressing. Since it had been late when he got back to the motel Friday night, he hadn't returned Vanessa's call. He had awakened Saturday morning to her loud knocking on his door. He let her in, then went in the bathroom to splash water on his face. He looked in the mirror and told himself not to show his irritation, but he really didn't appreciate her coming to his room like this. For one thing, it didn't look good. It seemed like her father would tell her things like that. Secondly, he liked to wake up each morning and have prayer time and read at least a verse or two of scripture. Oh well, next time he would know to return her call no matter how late it was.

Vanessa had a lot on her mind. She didn't know where to start complaining first. "What was the mess with the girl last night?" was the first question out of her mouth.

"Excuse me?" Levi asked.

"That was so obviously staged and fake. I didn't think you would stoop to such theatrics."

"Oh, so you think I found someone to come in and pretend to need prayer?"

"What else could it have been? I guess you're telling me you're a fortune teller?"

"You know, Vanessa, I don't really want to go there with you right now. If you were in the service last night and you didn't see what God did, I certainly can't stand here and try to explain it to you."

"Oh, so I wait up for you to call me back and you're the one that's going to have an attitude?"

"I don't have an attitude. I apologize for not getting back with you, but it was late when I got here, and I didn't want to wake everyone up."

"We weren't sleep. Where were you all of that time?"

"I went over to Mother Ingram's to talk to Sheba some more."

"Oh, so Sheba is more important to you than I am?"

"Her needs were more important at the time." Levi was trying desperately to hold on to his temper.

"I'll be so glad when you get the job at Glorious Morning. Now that's a real church."

"I'm going there tomorrow because I gave my word, but I know for a fact I won't be pastoring there."

"Oh, you'll get the job. It's just a formality having you preach tomorrow."

"Thanks for the vote of confidence, but even if they offer it to me, I'm not going to accept."

"What do you mean you're not going to accept? Why would you spend all of that time at the seminary if you don't plan to preach?"

"I do plan to preach, just not there."

"This is the second church you've turned down. What are you looking for?"

"I'm hoping to hear from Christ's Church.

"Please tell me you're joking." At his silence, Vanessa continued. "I can't believe you would turn down a successful church like Glorious Morning to go pastor those backward, ignorant people."

"Whoa, wait a minute. Why are they backward, ignorant people?"

"I didn't mean it like that. But Daddy's gone to a lot of trouble and..."

"What does your daddy have to do with this?"

"Nothing, I just meant coming up here with me and everything."

"No, you didn't. Your daddy arranged my little accidental meeting with Mr. McKoy didn't he?" Vanessa didn't answer, but the look on her face told Levi all he needed to know. "Vanessa, I'm talking to you. I'm asking you a question, and don't lie to me."

"Yes. But what's so wrong about that? Daddy pastored there before we moved to Atlanta."

"Oh, I see."

"Honey, please, let's discuss this. I think we would be so much happier at Glorious Morning."

"Vanessa, this is not about where I would be the happiest, although if the people are like the officers I met, I can't even imagine myself at Glorious Morning, much less imagine myself being happy there. I have to go where the Holy Spirit leads me."

"They probably can't even pay you enough to support yourself, let alone both of us. You know I like nice things."

"I can always do bookkeeping on the side like I do now."

"Levi, I don't know what's gotten into you, but if you take the job at Christ's Church, we're through. I am not going to be the first lady of a church like that. My daddy always discussed important issues like this with my mother first."

"I see. Then it's a good thing that we're having this discussion before I propose marriage then, isn't it? Because any woman I marry will have to understand that I have to obey the voice of God. And if He gives me a wife, surely He will give her the desire to go where He leads us. I don't know what kind of men you're used to dealing with, but I don't accept ultimatums. I'm telling you flat out, I'm not accepting a position at Glorious Morning, not to please you and not to please your daddy."

By this time Vanessa had resorted to tears and rushed from the room. While Levi was pondering whether to go after her, Rev. Hampton called and Levi agreed to meet him and take him over to Mother Ingram's. He knocked on Vanessa's door on his way to the elevator. An unsmiling Rev. Lamar opened the door and informed him that Vanessa did not wish to speak to him. Levi had asked him if he would like to ride with him and meet Rev. Hampton. Not to his surprise, Rev. Lamar refused and shut the door.

Chapter 21

Levi and Rev. Hampton hit it off from the start. Rev. and Mrs. Hampton, Perry and Mary, Mother Ingram, Sheba, Shalan, and Levi sat around talking for hours. Kendrick was spending the day with the younger Ingram couple. Shalan and Mary fixed a delicious supper for everyone. There was fried chicken, string beans seasoned with ham, corn on the cob, mashed potatoes and gravy, biscuits, apple pie, tea and lemonade.

"It's a good thing we decided to spend the night, honey," Rev. Hampton told his wife.

"After a meal like that I'm not good for anything except going to sleep."

"Why don't you go up and get some rest? I know you've got to be tired," Perry encouraged them. The Hamptons had had a tearful reunion with their daughter that morning and had been too excited to rest after getting there. They acknowledged that they were tired, and went up to the guest room. Sheba was going to sleep in Shalan's room, and Shalan would sleep with Kendrick. Rev. Hampton invited Levi to come preach at his church some time in the future and the two men exchanged phone numbers and email addresses. At one time during the day, the two men of God had walked around the block together. Levi had confided in him about his earlier exchange with Vanessa. He felt comfortable talking it over with someone who didn't know Vanessa. While Rev. Hampton didn't come right out and say that he and Vanessa weren't compatible, he asked Levi enough probing questions to make him come to that conclusion himself. It was as if a burden were lifted. Levi had wanted deep down inside to break it off with her. But he had been the "love them and leave them" type before he became a Christian. He didn't want to have that reputation as a man of God. Her parents had really been excited about the match. But in the end, he had to be true to himself. This was not a woman he would want to live with for the rest of his life. Levi was now practicing celibacy, and Vanessa had tried to use seduction more than once as a means to get a proposal from him. Yes, it was better to let her hate him now than to ruin both of their lives.

Just as he was getting ready to leave Mother Ingram's, Perry followed him outside. "In all of the excitement, I forgot to talk to you about your future plans. A lot of the members really liked you this week and wanted to know if you would consider being our pastor."

"Yes, sir. I would consider it. I would love to pastor your church."

"And the thing with Shalan? Did you two straighten that out?"

"Yes, we sure did."

"Okay, well, we'll have to take it through the proper channels. We'll probably have a congregation meeting later this month and put it to a vote, but I would advise you to start packing when you get home." The two men shook hands.

"Okay, I'll do that. And thanks for everything."

"No problem. You have a good night, now."

"You, too. Oh, one more thing. In case you hear it from somewhere else, I promised to speak at Glorious Morning tomorrow. But I'm not considering pastoring there."

"I appreciate you telling me. Good night."

"Good night." Levi's step was light as he walked to his rental car.

Chapter 22

When Levi got back to his room the message light was on. Thinking it was Vanessa or his mom, he listened to it. It was Mr. McKoy telling him that Rev. Lamar was going to deliver the message the next day and they wouldn't be needing him after all. Levi laughed out loud. He called the front desk to see if Vanessa and her parents had checked out. They had. He decided to use the indoor pool, then come back to the room and get some rest. Tomorrow, maybe he would visit Christ's Church.

Everyone was surprised to see him in church Sunday morning. One of the officers was prepared to bring a message, but when Levi came in he offered him the pulpit. "I just came to sit in," Levi told him. "My plans changed so I just wanted to worship with you, but you go ahead." Brother Brown did a good job speaking. He talked about the day of Pentecost, and got a lot of Amens. He then gave space for Levi to have a few words. Levi told him how much he had gotten out of his sermon, and thanked the congregation for their support during the revival. He surprised Shalan by saying that he had run into one of his former neighbors and friends at this church, Miss Shalan Sanders. He told them that he was going to have to leave in order to make his flight, but to keep him in their prayers.

On the way to the airport, Levi finally remembered to call home. First he called Angie and told her to get their mother on three-way. They were shocked, to say the least, when he told them about running into Shalan. He told them that it was a real possibility that he would be moving to Maryland. "Oh, and she has a little boy."

"What?"

"How old is he?"

"I don't know, maybe three."

"Is she married?"

"No."

"Did she meet someone in New York?"

"I think she said the father didn't live in New York. I didn't want to be too nosy."

"Since when?" questioned Angie.

"Is he cute?" asked his mother.

"Yeah, he is. In fact, come to think of it, he looks kind of like Rod did when he was little. Same color eyes…" His voice trailed off.

"Our *brother*, Rod?" asked Angie.

"Yeah."

"You don't think she and Hugh…?" asked Mrs. Leach.

"No, Momma, I don't. But look, I'm not going to make this flight. I need to go talk to Shalan."

"Call me," his mother said, understanding what he hadn't said.

"I will. I love you, Momma."

"I love you, too, Son."

"Love you, Brother."

"Love you, too. I'll call you." Levi took the next exit and turned around. How could he have been so stupid? The truth had been staring him right in the face. God, what she must have gone through—parents dead and thinking he didn't love her. Why hadn't she told him! Didn't she know that he would have been there?

Levi pulled up in front of Mother Ingram's house. *Okay, stay calm.* How was he going to manage a private conversation with Shalan? He went and rang the bell.

Mother Ingram came to the door.

"I thought you had a plane to catch."

"Yes, ma'am, but I decided to take a later flight. Uh, is Shalan here by any chance?"

"Yes, she just went to put Kendrick down for his nap. She'll be down in a few minutes. Can I get you something to eat or drink?"

"No, ma'am I'm fine. Did the Hamptons get off okay?"

"Yeah, they pulled out around nine this morning." Shalan walked in the room just then.

"Hi, Levi. I thought you were in the air by now."

"Yeah, something came up. I'm going to leave tonight. But I was wondering, do you have time to ride somewhere with me? That is if Mother Ingram could listen out for Kendrick for you? We won't be gone long."

"Take all the time you need. I'm not going anywhere, but on this couch," Mother Ingram told them.

"Is there a park where we can go talk?" Levi asked Shalan after they were in the car.

"Yeah, take the second right. What's going on?"

"I just need to talk to you." Levi pulled up to the neighborhood park and turned the switch off. Just for something to say, Shalan asked him if this was his car.

"No, it's a rental. Mine has seen better days, but that's the first thing I'm going to buy when I get a permanent job—a car. Shalan, I don't know any easy way to say this." He took a deep breath. "I think I know who Kendrick's daddy is. But if I'm wrong, tell me."

"How can I tell you if you're wrong when I don't know who you're thinking?"

"Shalan, look at me." She did, but couldn't hold his gaze. "Why didn't you tell me?"

Shalan started crying.

"Don't cry, baby. I'm not mad at you. I just need to know why."

"I didn't want to ruin your life."

"Ruin my life? Baby, back then you *were* my life."

"You were going in the ministry and I didn't want you to have to marry me when you were in love with someone else."

"I can't believe a phone call changed the course of my life. I told you the other day Ariana was not my girlfriend."

"I know that now, but I didn't then. I'm just telling you why I didn't tell you."

"Okay, it doesn't matter now. Now I know why God brought me here. Man, I have a son."

"How did you guess?"

"I was telling Momma and Angie about his eyes and saying that he reminds me of Rod." He laughed. "Momma thought you and Hugh had been fooling around."

"Did you tell her that you and I had?"

"I didn't have to. I just told them I was going to miss my flight and come talk to you. Tell me about the pregnancy and when he was born. Do you have any pictures I can have? When are you going to tell him about his daddy?"

"Okay, slow your roll. One question at a time."

They sat in the park for two hours, catching each other up. After the first 30 minutes, they got out of the car and walked to a nearby bench. They walked the trail twice. Levi told her about how he had wrestled with his decision over the two churches without telling her Vanessa's reaction. Shalan again told him that he needed to go where he could be free to use the gifts God had given him. "I'm glad you let the Holy Spirit lead you," she told him.

"I am, too, I just wanted to see what you thought about it." She looked at him in a puzzled way. "I guess I'd better take you home. You think Kendrick might be waking up now?"

"Yeah, probably. We've been gone for over two hours."

"Come on." He took her hand and held it as they walked back to the car. He opened her car door for her and closed it behind her. As he took his seat on the driver's side, he looked at her. "You know now that I've found you, I'm not letting you go again. In about six months, Mother Ingram might have to find someone else to live with her."

"Why is that?" she teased.

"Okay, play dumb, but you heard what I said."

"I told you you're full of yourself."

"No, I just know that God has given me the desires of my heart and I'm not going to mess up. I don't know about your love life and I don't even want to know, but I can look you in your eyes and tell you that I haven't been with anyone else since you. I promised God that I wouldn't make love to another woman unless she was my wife, and I've kept that promise. And I won't lie to you and say I haven't been tempted because I have. But you know it hasn't been as hard as I thought it would be. Maybe because I haven't loved anyone the way

I love you."

"You were in love with me?"

"Listen again. I haven't loved anyone the way I *love* you, present tense. Girl, I love you. I'm not saying that because we have a son, but I love you. Before I accept the job as pastor, I'm going to tell the officers the truth about Kendrick. I won't hide my son. I hope they understand, but if not, another door will open somewhere. I want us to be a family. I want to take you to dinner, to the movies, I want us to take Kendrick to the park, to the zoo, do the little family thang, ya know? I'm going to make you love me, because one day I'm going to ask you to be my wife."

"You don't have to make me love you, Levi. I already love you. I have for a long time. There hasn't been anyone for me either. I've been on a few dates but nothing serious. Oh, and I may as well tell you, I've been out with one of the guys at church a couple of times. Billy—you know, the guy that plays the keyboards?"

"Yeah. Do you know if he has any feelings for you?"

"I don't think so."

"Okay, baby, thanks for giving me a heads up on that. Who else knows that I'm Kendrick's father?"

"LaTia and Mother Ingram, Aunt Faye probably suspects."

"Mother Ingram!"

"Yep. She guessed the night I came home crying from the revival."

"Okay, well the whole church will know before long because we're going to tell them." He kissed her then and the years rolled away. With a final hug, he started the car and together they went to see their son.

Chapter 23

Levi had been the pastor of Christ's Church for two months. After that day in the park, he had turned the rental car in and stayed a few more days in Maryland. Rather than take a flight, he, Shalan, and Kendrick had driven her Explorer to North Carolina so that Kendrick could meet his grandparents and aunts and uncles. It was a joyous reunion. Levi had told his family up front that he didn't want anyone chastising Shalan for keeping Kendrick a secret. She may not have made the wisest decision, but she had done what she thought best at the time. Angie quickly asked her to be her maid of honor.

"But don't you already have one?"

"I have a matron of honor. So now I'll just have two honor attendants. I can't get married without my best friend up there beside me."

Shalan had hugged her to hide her tears. Hugh had gotten married in April, and Shalan met his wife, Delisa. She looked more like his sister than his wife. She teased him, telling him he tried to find someone who looked like his mother. She was going to be one of Angie's bridesmaids. "I need to find another flower girl now because you know I've got to let my nephew be one of my ring bearers." Angie picked him up for another kiss.

Later that night as most of the family gathered in the family room, Shalan sought out Will and Linda Leach. She found them in the kitchen having a cup of coffee. "Hi," she said a bit nervously. "Am I interrupting anything?"

"No, no," Linda assured her. "Have a cup of coffee with us."

"Okay. Don't get up, I'll get it." Shalan had only been in their home a few times after they moved and didn't feel as comfortable as she had in their old home. After looking through a few cabinets, she found the coffee mugs and poured herself a cup. She sat down at the table with the two people who would probably be her in-laws, feeling more uncomfortable than she ever had in their presence.

"Is something bothering you, Shalan?" Will asked.

"No. Yes." She took a deep breath. "I just wanted to apologize to both of you."

Shalan put her head down and started crying. Linda went and knelt down beside her chair.

"Shalan, you don't owe us an apology." She put her arms around the younger woman.

"I kept your only grandchild away from you," Shalan managed to say through her tears.

"Levi explained everything to us. And, honey, we understand. No one is mad at you. We're all just sorry that you had to go through all of that by yourself." Linda was crying, too.

"I wanted to call you so many times, but I didn't want Levi to hate me."

"Levi wouldn't have hated you, you know that now, don't you?" Shalan nodded.

Will added, "The important thing is that you and Kendrick are with us now. If there's anything at all we can do for either one of you, you know all you have to do is ask."

"Yes, sir."

"Hey, I was wondering where you disappeared to," Levi said, coming in the kitchen. "You okay, babe?"

"Yeah, I was just talking to your folks." Levi noticed the tears, but didn't comment.

"You aren't letting her get too far out of your sight, are you, Son?" Will teased.

"Nope. We're about to play Scrabble, you want to play?"

"Yeah, I guess so." Levi sat with them as they finished their coffee. Will met his wife's eye as they silently communicated the way couples do when they have been together for a long time.

Our son is in love.

Yes, look at the way he looks at her. Looks like we're going to have another daughter-in-law soon.

Uh-huh.

Shalan smiled as she thought back to that time. It was November now and the family was coming here for Thanksgiving. Then next month they would make the trip to North Carolina for Christmas and the wedding. Shalan couldn't think of a time when she had been happier. True to his word, Levi had told the officers of the church about Kendrick, and it had not made a difference to them. Shalan had prepared Kendrick before she let Levi come in. "So is my daddy mean?" had been his first question. Shalan had assured him that Daddy wasn't himself the night he had hurt her feelings. After Levi moved to Maryland, the two of them had taken Kendrick on outings together the first few times. Then Levi had asked if she thought he was ready to come spend some time alone with him. Since then he had spent either a Friday or a Sunday night with him almost every week.

The members of Christ's Church had truly grown to love Levi. The young people said he believed in "keeping it real." He enjoyed shooting hoops with them in back of the church, but he also gave them a seasoned answer in the things of the Lord. One of the guys who had attended revival asked him if he broke up with Vanessa to be with Shalan. Levi had answered him in an honest way telling him that while Vanessa was a sweet person she was not the woman the Lord had ordained him to be with. He told the guy that it was God's will that he come to Maryland when he did because Shalan and Kendrick were there. Another of the boys asked what he thought of premarital sex.

Levi knew the rest of the guys were listening to see what his answer would be, especially since they knew about Kendrick. He told them that before he became saved he saw nothing wrong with having sex as long as the girl was willing. He told them that he and his friends had sex with girls that they had no feelings for, and that alone was wrong.

However, when he accepted Christ in his life, he realized that it was God's perfect plan that a couple refrain from having sex whether they loved one another or not, until they become man and wife. In the case with Shalan, he had yielded to temptation because of the love he felt for her. "I knew it was wrong even at the time, but I was thinking *I've been with those other girls I didn't love, so maybe just one time won't hurt.* But in the end, I hurt Shalan and myself, too, because she walked out of my life. But the good news..."

The boys started laughing and saying, "Here comes the preaching moment."

Levi laughed, too. "Well I am a preacher after all. But seriously, the good news is that God is a God of second chances. And all, things work together for good for those of us who love the Lord." The boys were quiet and reflective for a few minutes until Levi said, "Play ball."

Delisa had called with the news that she was pregnant the same week Kara Ingram announced that she was pregnant. Shalan thought that once she and Levi were married, she would like to have a least one more child. Speaking of getting married, this email she was reading might be the answer to her prayers. She had prayed that Mother Ingram wouldn't be alone once she got married. Today she had received an email from Sheba Hampton saying that she wanted to come live up here. The two of them emailed one another almost on a daily basis. The guy that had threatened her life was dead. One of his enemies had posted bail for him. When he walked out of jail, not knowing who had posted bail, he had been gunned down. Even though he had threatened Sheba, the news had still shaken her up. The good news was that she was back on track with her walk with the Lord. She just wanted a change of pace. Shalan made a mental note to talk to Mother Ingram about it before answering the email. Maybe she should wait until Levi proposed before she started giving her room away. Of course there was an extra room she reasoned.

Chapter 24

The only dark cloud on Levi's horizon these days were two feuding gangs with church ties. The leader of one gang was grandson to one of the mothers of the church. The other leader had a brother who had started coming to the church. He idolized Levi and wanted him to help his brother. He confided that his mother couldn't handle him anymore, and their dad wasn't in the picture.

"Where does your dad live?"

"Oh, he lives in Virginia, but he's married with two other kids and he just doesn't have much to do with us. Make that nothing to do with us."

"Okay, Jamal, here's what I'm going to do. First I'm going to pray and ask God for direction. I'm going to ask some of my prayer warriors to pray about the situation as well. When I get the nod from Heaven, I'm going to talk to your brother." He saw the look of expectancy on Jamal's face. "Let me just tell you one thing, though. God's time is not always like our time. It may take some weeks or months before I talk to your brother, or it may be tomorrow. But I give you my word and my word is my bond, I will talk to him. Okay?"

"Thank you, Pastor."

"And Jamal, one thing I want you to promise me. If you feel yourself getting tempted to join, I want you to call me. I don't care what time of the day or night it is. Will you promise me that?"

"Yes, but I'm not going to join. No way."

Levi spent the rest of the day in prayer. That night he called Shalan and asked her to fast with him the next day as they sought the Lord for direction. He also called Rev. Hampton down in South Carolina and asked the same of him. Rev. Hampton called Sheba to the phone to answer some questions that Levi had about gangs. She told him that once you were a part of one it was hard to break away from it. Sometimes you were threatened if you tried to get out. Also, most gangs that she knew about made you do some type of criminal activity to get initiated. That way they had something to hold over you if you tried to get out.

After hanging up the phone, Levi just sat and thought of the waste of so many young lives; he especially felt a burden for the young black brothers. So many were getting killed before they had a chance to really experience life. Then there were those filling up the prisons because of murder and drugs. "God if I can just help one brother see that if he wants to be a businessman, be a legitimate businessman! I'm tired of young people throwing their lives away. God, and if I can just help them to seek comfort in your house, Lord, and not in some gang! Lord, you sent me here, now tell me what you would have me do. I told you once before, Lord, you've got to help a brother out."

Chapter 25

Thanksgiving was truly a day of giving thanks. All six Leach siblings were there along with their parents. Angie's fiancé and his parents were there also. Delisa's grandparents had raised her, and since they were deceased now, she was happy to be part of the Leach family. Kendrick had spent Wednesday night, and had delighted in all of the attention. The manse had two bedrooms, a bath, and a wide hall upstairs. Downstairs was another bathroom, a bedroom with a half bath, a living room, kitchen, and dining room. It was a lot of house for one man Levi often thought. The church had bought it at a steal since it needed so much TLC. The men of the church had lovingly restored it and it was truly a beautiful home. He looked forward to having Shalan and Kendrick here with him once they were married. Last night was the first night the house had been full since Levi had moved in. He had put his parents in his bedroom with Kendrick happily in between them, Angie's future in-laws slept in one of the upstairs bedrooms, and the young women—Angie, Delisa, and his sister, Pamela—had taken the other bedroom. The men had roughed it, sleeping on the floor in sleeping bags or if you got to it first, a couch.

It had been like old times. Levi hadn't realized how much he missed his family until they were all together again. Shalan had stayed until 11:00 and had come back around 11:00 the next morning to help with the meal and just to be in their midst.

Levi had invited Mother Ingram and her family over, but they had declined. Her other sons and their families were coming down, so both households were going to have plenty of mouths to feed. Levi and Shalan had estimated they would have 14 mouths to feed. The dining room table held six, but they figured they could squeeze 8 at the table.

They thought about bringing the kitchen table in there, but then decided to put the food on the kitchen table and let everyone serve himself buffet style before sitting down. They put two card tables together and got folding chairs so everyone could sit in the dining room at the same time and eat together. Levi asked his dad to bless the food, which he did and at the same time thanked God for a day when all of his children were together and well and he thanked him also for the additions to the family. Everyone held hands and said one thing they were thankful for. This had been a Leach tradition for as long as the children could remember. When it was Levi's turn, he said he was thankful for finding the love of his life again and the little person in the room. "Who's the little person, Daddy?" asked Kendrick innocently.

"You are, Son."

"Oh, you mean 'cause I'm your little boy?"

"Exactly." Levi smiled at him.

When it was Shalan's turn, she declared that she couldn't narrow it down to one thing. "I'm thankful for my church family, for being with y'all again, I'm thankful for the Ingram family being a part of my life, I'm thankful that God saved me, and I'm thankful for Kendrick and Levi."

Levi smiled across the table at her. After dinner, the men retired to the living room to watch football. The women made quick work of cleaning the kitchen, with everyone pitching in. "So," Angie asked, "what are we going to do? Watch football with the men, or what?"

"Let's go in Levi's room and watch movies," Mrs. Leach suggested.

"Excuse me, ladies." It was Levi.

"Yes, may we help you?" asked Angie.

"Actually you can. I just put Kendrick down for a nap. I was wondering if I could get you to listen out for him. I need to show Shalan something. We won't be gone for more than an hour."

"I thought you were watching football," Pamela said.

"See, that's what I keep telling you. Don't think. You don't do it very well."

"Oh, shut up."

"Shut don't go up."

"All right, children, am I going to have to get my belt?" Mrs. Leach went along with their clowning.

"Come on, Shalan. Get your coat before Momma gives me a whipping."

"Where are we going?" asked Shalan as they walked to the car.

"Women and their questions. You can't wait and see, can you?"

"No."

"Okay, we're going to the park near your house to talk. Is that okay with you?"

"Yes. What's so important though that we had to leave the house like that?"

"Baby, if I had wanted to discuss it before we got to the park, we wouldn't be going to the park, now would we? Just hold your little horses."

Shalan didn't say anything else but her mind was going through possibilities. Maybe it was something with the gang thing. She knew Levi was about ready to move on that.

Levi parked the car and left it running. He put on a CD. The Four Tops were singing *I Believe In You and Me*. "First on the agenda, how about a kiss?" Shalan leaned over and they kissed. "Whoever dreamed up bucket seats needs a kick in the seat," Levi complained. He got out of the car, walked around to the passenger side and opened the door. Taking Shalan by the hand, he helped her out of the car. He then proceeded to kiss her with his arms holding her tightly. "Now that's more like it, but get back in the car. I can't take too much of that."

After he got back in, he just sat for a few minutes. Then he turned to her. "Shalan, I was going to wait until Christmas to ask you this, but sitting across the table from you today, I realized I don't want to wait another day. I love you very much and you're everything and more than I ever wanted in a woman, in a wife. Baby, will you marry me?"

Shalan started to cry. She had always cried easily when she was emotional.

"Is that a yes cry or a no cry?"

"Yes, yes, yes."

"Thank you, Jesus. I feel badly, though. I don't have your ring. I hadn't planned to do this today."

"That's okay."

"I'll come pick you up tomorrow, and we'll go look, okay?"

"We can wait. I know you want to spend time with your family."

"No, we're going tomorrow. Mom and Angie and Pamela are going shopping as soon as the stores open. You know how they are about the day after Thanksgiving."

"What about Delisa?"

"She and Hugh are going to Silver Spring to visit one of her cousins. I'm going to ask Dad to watch Kendrick. Then I'll have them meet us somewhere for lunch."

"Okay."

"Shalan."

"Yes?"

"Do you love me?"

"Yes, you know I do."

"I mean we've always loved each other, but I guess I'm asking are you sure you're in love with me?"

"Yes, Levi, I'm in love with you."

"That's good, because I am so in love with you that sometimes I want to just stop and tell somebody. Baby, I'm going to do everything I can to make you happy."

"I *am* happy. I just wish Momma and Daddy could have lived to see me get married."

Levi reached across the seat and held her. "I know, baby. I miss them, too. But you know what? I'll bet they knew before we did that we would end up together someday."

"You think so?"

"Um huh. My family didn't see it coming because we were never alone around them. But the night I took you to the prom, I saw a secret look pass between them like they knew we had feelings for each other but didn't know it yet. It was kind of a knowing look." They sat, each lost in thought for a few minutes. Levi, anxious to break his news, backed the car up. "Okay, what are we going to say?"

"I'm not saying anything," Shalan declared. "This is your ball game."

"Speaking of ball games, I guess I'll have to wait for a commercial to tell my dad."

"I can't believe you left the game to propose. You must love me," Shalan teased.

"More than you know," Levi answered seriously.

Chapter 26

When they opened the front door, everyone was in the living room. "Okay, where's the ring?" Pamela asked.

"What ring?" Levi looked puzzled. Pamela went and looked at Shalan's hand.

She reached in her pocket and got a $5 bill out.

"I bet Angie that you had gone off to propose." She handed the money to a smirking Angie.

"I can't believe you two heathens are betting in my house." Levi started clowning. He shook his head. "The house where the servant of God lays his head."

"Say so, Preacher. Amen." Rod, Hugh, and Greg backed him up.

"The Devil is busy."

"Yes he is."

"When the good man leaves the house, the Devil wants to come in and take over."

"Yes he does."

"Y'all are too silly," Angie said.

"And anyway," Levi said, still acting as if he were preaching, "Ms. Angie Leach soon to be Reed, you need to give your sister her $5 back and give her $5 out of your pocket, because I asked the woman to marry me and she said yes. Can I get an Amen?"

"Amen!" everyone in the room answered. Then there was hugging and congratulations all around.

Chapter 27

Meanwhile, at the Ingram household, the sons were discussing Sheba Hampton. "I'm just not sure about her moving here with Momma," Ralph said. "Perry, you said yourself she's been mixed up with gangs. Was she on drugs?"

"I can't honestly say she wasn't; I don't know. She didn't seem to be on any when she was here. But I would bet my life that she's not on any now. The guy she was with is dead now. After what he put her through, I don't think she'll go that route again."

"Still, you never know," argued Marlon.

"You're right. We didn't know anything about Shalan when she moved in either. Mama's not senile. If things aren't right, she'll be the first to say something. And you two are forgetting, I'm over here several times a week, and if I'm not, Mary or one of the kids is over here."

"Well, Shalan's not moving out for a while yet, is she?" asked Ralph. At Perry's shake of the head, he proposed that Sheba move in on a trial basis. "That way it will give Mama and Sheba both a chance to back out if things aren't working out."

"Oh, this might make you feel better," Perry told them. "You know Kara and Travis are expecting?" His two brothers nodded. "They want to move out of their apartment before the baby's born. That house down the street is going on the market next week. The guy who owns it told me he's going to sell it after he does a little work on it. I told Mary I would be willing to put the down payment on it so Kara and Travis can get it. That way if Mama is by herself one night she could go there and spend the night or they could come up here and check on her."

"Yeah, that sounds good. If you need help with the down payment call me," Marlon told him. "You don't even have to pay it back. It'll make me sleep better knowing family is in the neighborhood since Mama refuses to move in with one of us."

"Oh, she did say she was going to come spend two weeks in New York this summer," Ralph told his brother. They lived blocks from each other in Brooklyn. They had just turned their attention back to the game when they heard their mother squeal.

Ralph and Marlon jumped up, looking alarmed. Perry calmed them down. "That's her happy squeal." They went in the kitchen where Kara and Travis had gone just minutes before. They had spent the day with Kara's family, but Travis had saved room for his grandmother's sweet potato pie. Travis was sitting at the table with pie a la mode.

"Shalan just got engaged. That's what all of the squealing is about. Kara's going to be a bridesmaid." Travis delivered the news as though it wasn't as exciting as the pie he was eating.

"When's the wedding?" asked Perry.

"In April," answered Mother Ingram. "She wants me to sit on the bride's side of the family on the front row." Mother Ingram wiped tears from her eyes. "I'm so happy for her, but I sure am going to miss her."

"We were just thinking about what would happen if Shalan moved out," Perry told her. "Do you still want Sheba to move in?"

"Yes, why wouldn't I? She's coming right before Christmas when her daddy comes to preach." Levi had arranged with Rev. Hampton to preach for him the Sunday after Angie's wedding. The older man had agreed and insisted that the church not pay him. He and his wife would bring Sheba and help her get settled in. His associate pastor would take over in his absence. Since Shalan would be in North Carolina, Mother Ingram had insisted that the Hamptons stay at her house.

Chapter 28

That night when Shalan came home, she and Mother Ingram discussed wedding plans. She wanted her attendants to wear lavender. She knew that much.

"How many do you plan to have?"

"Let's see. Angie will be married then, so she'll be my matron of honor. Pamela, Levi's other sister will be a bridesmaid, Kara…" Oh, no, I promised LaTia she could be my matron of honor. I had no idea I'd be marrying Levi. What should I do, Mother Ingram?"

"Which one is more understanding?"

"Angie, but Angie's my best friend!"

"Well, who says you can't have two? It's your wedding."

"I might do that. Okay, bridesmaids, Kara, Pamela, Sherise—she's the girl I eat lunch with at work—Sheba, and Alisa. Alisa's my girlfriend from New York, oh and my college roommate, how many is that?"

"Six bridesmaids and two matrons of honor. When is Kara due?"

"Oh yeah, I forgot she's pregnant. I think the baby's due around May. Do you think I should ask Delisa? She's pregnant, too." Maybe we need to postpone the wedding until June." She picked up the phone and called Levi. After explaining the situation to him there was silence for a minute.

"Okay, you have three choices, have two very pregnant bridesmaids in the wedding, have two very pregnant friends sitting in the pews, or move the wedding up. No way am I moving it back."

"Okay, how about Valentine's Day? What day is that on?"

"I have no idea. Just let me know what time to be at the church."

"You are such a big help."

"Thank you. I love you and good night."

"Did I wake you up?"

"Yeah but that's alright. You need to get some rest yourself. I'll see you in the morning."

"Oh, wait, Levi."

"Yes, honey?"

"Kendrick's birthday is the 17th. Maybe we should wait until after then."

"No, we'll just go on a two-day honeymoon and have a party for him when we get back."

"Okay."

"I don't want to be away from him much longer than that anyway."

"Okay, you're so sweet."

"That's why you love me."

"Uh huh."

"Uh huh what?"

"That's why."

"Oh, somebody's listening and you don't want to tell your man you love him?" he teased.

"Yeeees."

"Well, I'm not going to hang up until you tell me."

"I thought you were so sleepy."

"I just got refreshed."

"Yes, that's a definite."

"I'm waiting."

Shalan lowered her voice. "I love you."

"Now that wasn't so hard, was it?"

"Good night." Levi laughed and hung up.

With her face feeling warm, Shalan hung up the phone and turned back to Mother Ingram. "Okay, Mother Ingram. We need to think red instead of lavender and I need one more bridesmaid to make it an even number in case I ask Delisa." Mother Ingram just smiled. It was good to see Shalan so animated. Things had really turned around in such a short time.

Chapter 29

Levi parked his car outside of the apartment complex where Jamal lived with his mother and brother, Jalen. He had told Jamal to call him sometime when Jalan was home so that he could meet him. Jamal and Jalan were going to be outside shooting hoops when Levi "happened" to drop by. He had thought about wearing his sneakers, but thought that would be too obvious. If invited to play, he would go to the car and get them. He walked over to the enclosed court where Jamal and several other boys were playing. It was easy to pick Jalan out. He looked a lot like his brother, only more streetwise. The brothers were about the same height and coloring, but Jalan already had a man's body. Jamal looked up and noticed Levi standing there. "Hey, Pastor," he greeted him. "Hold up a minute," he told the other boys in the game. They looked curiously at Levi as Jamal came over to him.

"Yo, you gonna play ball or what?" Jalan asked his brother, rudely.

"Hold up, man, this is my pastor."

"Well this ain't church," Jalan replied.

"It's okay," Levi told Jamal, "go ahead; I'll wait here."

While the game was in progress, Levi talked silently to God asking for a way to get through to the young man. After the game was over, Jalan put a towel around his neck and started to walk off in the opposite direction. "Hey, Jalan, wait up," Levi called out to him.

"Hey, man, how you know my name?"

Jamal talks about you a lot and I could see right away how much the two of you look alike."

"Oh yeah? So what kind of things has my brother been saying about me to you that would be any of your business?"

"Oh, nothing specific, you know, just conversation."

"So what brings you over here?"

"I get out and shoot with the boys at the church sometimes, and Jamal's been telling me about the court near his house so I just decided to come check it out."

Jalan looked at him suspiciously.

"So you try to play a little?"

Levi said, "Yeah, sure do. You got some mad skills there, man, reminds me of myself when I was your age."

"Oh, so you trying to tell me you used to play like me?"

"Exactly."

"And you still trying to play as long as the competition is weak?"

"Oh, if I'm playing, I want the competition to bring it."

"So what's up, you trying to challenge me or something?"

"No, are you trying to challenge me?"

"Naw, I don't want to embarrass you out here in front of my brother. That's all he talks about is Pastor this and Pastor that. 'Sides you don't have the right shoes."

"Oh, I can get some shoes. But don't let me embarrass you in front of your boys."

"Oh, a little psychology going on, huh?"

"No, I'm just saying I can back up what I say."

"Okay, put your money where your mouth is. One on one, first one to get to 15 pays up."

"Sorry, but I don't bet like that. Tell you what, though. If I beat you, how about coming to church with your brother Sunday?"

"See, you preachers are all alike. I knew you didn't 'just drop by.'"

"But if you think you can beat me, you don't have anything to lose, do you?"

"Oh, I know I can beat you. I just don't appreciate being set up."

"Come on, man. You know you weren't set up. I just complimented you on your skills and you took it from there. You issued a challenge; I just upped the ante a little. So what's up?"

"All right, but if I win, Jamal doesn't come to church Sunday."

Levi didn't hesitate. "No, I'm not going for that. You have to play for something that involves you, not Jamal."

"Umm, okay, when I win, emphasis on when, you have to treat all of us out here to dinner at Elaine's." Elaine's was a restaurant in the heart of the black community that specialized in soul food. The prices were reasonable and the food was delicious.

"Okay, I can handle that. Where can I change clothes? I have my gym bag in the car."

"Take him up to the crib, 'Mal." Levi followed Jamal up to the second floor of the building. His mother, a young-looking 36-year-old woman, was watching the news.

"Moms, this is my pastor, Pastor Levi." Jamila Woods stood and shook hands with Levi.

"Finally I get to meet the man that walks on water. Jamal talks about you all the time."

"I don't walk on water, but I'm glad that Jamal looks up to me. He's a good kid. I'm trying to teach him and the other young people to put their faith in the One who could walk on water."

"Uh huh."

"I apologize for not getting by here to meet you sooner. I know you've probably been concerned about what kind of teaching Jamal is getting at Christ's Church, but feel free to drop by any time."

"Thank you, I'm going to have to do that one of these Sundays."

"Jalan and I are going to do a little one-on-one, is it all right if I change clothes?"

"Sure. Jamal, show him the bathroom." Their apartment was small, but neat. The living and dining area was one huge room, with a small kitchen in the corner of the dining area. As he walked down the short hallway to the bathroom, Levi noticed the open door of Jamila's room. The door at the end of the hallway was closed, and he guessed Jamila kept it closed to keep from arguing with her sons about the mess. The bathroom was neat and was decorated with pictures and flowers. He had noticed pictures of the boys in the living room. All in all it looked like a home where there was love. He wondered what had caused Jalan to go astray. Maybe his mother had to work a lot and Jamal had said the father was out of the picture. He quickly changed into his basketball shorts, t-shirt, and sneakers. On the way out he thanked Jamila and told her he was looking forward to seeing her in church soon.

Chapter 30

Back on the court, Jalan asked, "You didn't try to hit on my moms, did you?"

Levi started to say that he didn't date older women, but he decided to go another route. "No, I'm engaged, but she is a pretty woman. I'm surprised she's still single."

"Yeah, well, some brothers don't want to raise somebody else's kids, and I know I wasn't trying to have some man who wasn't my daddy telling me what to do."

"Even if he was telling you the right things?"

"Look, you gonna play ball or preach?" Levi grinned at him, taking him by surprise.

"Right now we're going to play ball, I'll preach to you Sunday."

"Whatever." Levi knew that beating Jalan wasn't going to be easy, because he really was good. *But, Lord, you're on my side, right*? Levi questioned silently. The game went down to the wire with Levi winning by two points. The other boys looked on in awe. Levi put his hands on his knees, trying to get his breath. He exaggerated how tired he was to make Jalan feel better. "I got to hand it to you, man, you made me work for it. Tell you what, I'm hungry. How about we all go down to Elaine's anyway? My treat."

"Naw, man, you won. My word's my bond. I'll be in church Sunday."

"That's good to hear, but I still want to go to Elaine's." There were six boys standing around. "We can't all fit in my car, though."

"Jalan has a car," Jamal volunteered.

"Okay. Anyone who wants to go, come on. Jalan, if it'll make you feel better, you can pay for yours." Jamal and his two friends got in with Levi. The other two who were undoubtedly friends of Jalan got in with him. When they got to Elaine's, Levi called her to the side.

"Look, I have $20 on me, but I'm trying to reach these guys. Could you let me run through here tomorrow and pay you the difference and don't give me away?"

"Yeah, if I can't trust a preacher, I don't guess I can trust anybody." They enjoyed a chuckle. Levi was in there several times a week for lunch and sometimes for supper when he didn't eat at Mother Ingram's. Sometimes he, Shalan, and Kendrick came here for supper. "So did you and Shalan set a date yet?"

"Yeah, it's going to be a Valentine's wedding. Hey, maybe we can get you to cater it."

"You'd better talk to Shalan about that, but I'll be glad to help if I can."

"Okay, I'll see if she's already talked to someone." The guys and Levi sat in Elaine's for about an hour. Levi didn't push the conversation to talk about the things of the Lord, but even so, the boys could see Christ in him. Jalan's cell phone rang several times throughout the meal. He mostly ignored it. The last time it rang, he glanced at the caller ID and picked it up. After an urgent-sounding conversation, he said he had to roll.

"Thanks for dinner, Rev." He asked the two boys that had ridden with him if they could find a ride home. Before they could even answer, he was gone.

"I'll see to it that you get home," Levi told them. He had assumed that these guys were part of Jalan's gang, but apparently that wasn't the case. Jamal looked downhearted after Jalan left. Levi made two trips transporting the boys home. When he got home, he called Shalan and told her about his evening. She told him that she would continue to pray with him. Kendrick was already asleep, so he didn't get to tell him good night. After a shower, he read his Bible, then sat on the porch far into the night searching for answers.

The following Sunday, Jalan was not in the congregation at Christ's Church; however, Jamila Woods was.

Chapter 31

Levi still had not met Mother Pearl's grandson, KJ, the other young man he had been praying for. The day before he left to go to Angie's wedding, he decided to visit Mother Pearl and maybe meet her grandson. He had been told that KJ was 20, two years older than Jalan. Mother Pearl had raised KJ from infancy. Levi wasn't sure if the parents were dead or just absent from his life. He did know from comments that Mother Pearl had made that KJ did not have a job—not a legitimate one anyway. She said he always seemed to have money, though. She suspected his girlfriends were giving him money, but Levi suspected that he had another source, too. KJ answered the knock on the door. He was as tall as Levi and had on baggy pants, and a sweater with a matching doo rag. He wore Timberlands with the laces undone. "Yeah?" was his greeting.

"Hey, I was wondering if your grandmother is in? I'm her pastor, Levi Leach, and you must be KJ." KJ just looked at him for a few seconds before commanding him to "wait here." Levi stood on the porch and waited. KJ came back and reluctantly invited him in. KJ started back to his room, but Mother Pearl called him back.

"Sit in here with us for a few minutes, KJ."

"Aw, Grandma, I got things to do."

"What things? Like take out the trash, clean your room?" KJ sat down with one leg stretched out looking bored.

"What does KJ stand for?" Levi asked, just to start a conversation.

"Kendrick Joseph," his grandmother answered, then added to K.J, "Pastor Leach's son is named Kendrick, too."

"Lovely," muttered KJ under his breath. Mother Pearl and Levi carried the conversation from there, mostly ignoring KJ's presence. Every now and then Levi would try to draw him into the conversation, with no results. After a few minutes, the young man got up and went to his room. This time, Mother Pearl didn't try to stop him. Levi and Mother Pearl talked about Rev. Hampton and his family coming the following Sunday, and the fact that Sheba would be staying. Mother Pearl talked about how God had worked a miracle in that child's life.

"Yes, he did," agreed Levi. "It was through the testimonies that God first spoke to her." Levi shared what Sheba had told Shalan through their emails.

"That's why I hate it when people use testimony time as a time to vent their frustrations with other saints and not to glorify God," Levi continued. "It's a time to share what God has done for you, not to beat somebody else up for not testifying."

"Amen to that," Mother Pearl agreed.

"Well, I'm going to get out of here. I've got some more packing to do. I just wanted to come by and see you before I left."

"Well, I'm glad you did."

"You don't have to get up, Mother Pearl, I can see myself out." As Levi walked to the door he saw KJ standing in the hallway right outside the living room. He wondered how long he had been standing there. "It was nice meeting you, KJ."

KJ muttered an answer that Levi didn't catch. At least he now had a face to go with the young man that he had laid before the Lord so many nights for.

Chapter 32

It was good to be home again! They arrived in Sanford on Christmas Eve. Since Christmas had fallen on a Sunday this year, the congregation had elected to have service Christmas Eve and not hold a Sunday morning service. Shalan and Levi arrived just as the family was returning from the service. On Christmas morning everyone watched Kendrick tear into his gifts. Also waiting to be loaded in the SUV was a shiny red tricycle with a personalized license plate. For Shalan, Levi had gotten an angel to add to her collection. "Oh she's beautiful!" The angel was dressed in an off-white dress with lavender and green trim and a pillbox hat to match.

"That's not all," Levi told her when she started to get up to get his gift. He gave her two small packages. In one box was a family ring with all three of their birthstones, the other box was an anklet with an S on it.

"Thank you, darling." Shalan looked at him with undisguised love in her eyes. "Do I get a kiss?" She looked around at the rest of the family, who were exclaiming over their gifts. She quickly gave Levi a kiss on the cheek.

"Okay, everybody listen up!" Levi shouted. "Does anyone mind if Shalan gives me a kiss?"

"NO."

"You are so embarrassing."

"Okay, I'm embarrassing and my sister already told me I was silly. You sure you want to marry me?"

"Yes, I'm sure." He leaned forward and planted a kiss on her lips.

Then for her ears only, he whispered, "I'll be so glad when February 14th gets here. I love you, baby."

"I love you, too. Let me get your present from under the tree." She had gotten him an Atlanta Braves jacket.

The days leading up to the wedding were filled with visiting old friends. When Shalan took Kendrick by Miss Frances' house, the older woman had hugged him to her bosom and cried. "Girl, I ought to spank you for leaving and not letting anyone know where you were! Where is that Levi?"

"He has a lot of running to do, but he's going to pick us up. He'll come in and speak to you."

"He'd better, many times as y'all cut across my yard. I figured one day you'd end up with Levi."

"Really? You never thought I'd end up with Hugh?"

"No. I used to sit at your house and watch Levi watch you when he thought no one was looking. And I used to watch your face light up when he came in a room. I said to myself, those two will end up together or my name isn't Frances."

Later that afternoon, Levi took Shalan to visit her parents' graves. He and Kendrick went back to the car to give her a few moments alone. "Hey, you guys. Last time I was here I told you that I was pregnant. Well I guess you know, I have a son, and I'm going to marry his daddy soon. I miss you two so much, but now I have hope because I've gotten saved since I was here before. And I know that one day I'm going to see you again. I wish you could be at my wedding. Oh, Daddy, you won't get to walk me down the aisle! But I know you're in a better place. I still love you both. Bye now."

Shalan wiped tears from her eyes as she went to rejoin her men. "Are you sad, Mommy?"

"Just a little, honey. I miss my momma and daddy."

"Aren't they in Heaven?"

"Yes."

"Well, don't cry, they're probably happy up there. And you're happy down here with me and Daddy, right?" Shalan and Levi shared a smile above his head.

"Right, Son."

Chapter 33

Angie's wedding was lovely. Shalan didn't feel the sadness that had overshadowed LaTia's wedding for her because this time she realized that the next wedding she participated in would be hers. She looked across and met Levi's eyes. He gave her his famous wink.

The day after the wedding, Levi, Shalan, and Kendrick accompanied Mr. and Mrs. Leach to church. It was so good to see everyone again. It was Youth Sunday, and Miss Shelia was still in charge of the choir, only now younger children sang in the choir along with the teenagers. When it was time to do the pre-sermon selection, Miss Shelia got up and announced that two of her former choir members were in the congregation. She asked them if they would come up and do a selection following the choir's selection. Levi started to shake his head, but the congregation burst into applause. He and Shalan had never sung a duet before. "What are we going to sing?" he whispered while the choir was singing.

"How about 'Because of Who You Are' by Vickie Yohe?" Levi frowned and opened his mouth to object.

"Don't even try it, Levi."

"What?" he whispered back.

"You're always humming it, so don't say you don't know it."

That's what I get for loving a woman who knows me too well.

Shalan sang the first two lines, then Levi joined in. Their voices blended together perfectly as they lifted their hands in praise. The congregation was soon on its feet with some people lifting their hands, some humming or singing along, and some in tears. When they had finished, Shalan took the microphone. "Hallelujah, thank you, Jesus. It's so good to be home again. No matter where I go, this will always be home. And I just want to give God the praise because of who he is! Not because of what he's done for me, not for how far he's brought me from, not for all his blessings, but today I just want to praise Him for who He is."

All over the church you could hear someone cry out Amen, Hallelujah, or Thank you, Jesus, as the couple took their seats. Rev. McLean took the pulpit and gave a powerful sermon. Levi felt good just sitting back and listening to the Word. He made a vow to himself that any Sunday he wasn't in the pulpit, he was going to be in church somewhere listening to the Word. It was New Year's Day—the start of a brand new year. Life was good. Early in the morning he would take his son and his future wife back to Maryland. The church had been good to give him this time off, but it was time to go back. They had been gone for over a week.

After church they stood around being congratulated on their upcoming wedding. They had sent an invitation to the church and several people were going to come up. Right before they started out the door, someone came out of the office and told Levi he had an emergency phone call. Levi rushed to the office to take the call, Shalan on his heels.

After he hung up, he told her they needed to leave for Maryland within the next half-hour. "Is it Mother Ingram?" Shalan could tell from Levi's end of the conversation that someone was in intensive care.

"No, it's Mother Pearl. Her grandson asked that I be called." They went by the Leach household long enough to get their bags. Mrs. Leach packed some sandwiches for them to eat on the way, and Levi grabbed a few drinks out of the fridge. Soon they were headed north. Levi used his cell phone to call the hospital. He asked for the ICU waiting room. After a volunteer located KJ for him, he told him that they were on their way, and to hang in there.

Chapter 34

Shalan called Kara and asked her to meet them at the hospital so that she could take Kendrick home with her. She guessed rightly that Mother Ingram would be at the hospital. Levi and Shalan went straight to the waiting room before asking to see Mother Pearl. Mother Ingram hugged the two of them and told them that KJ was standing at the end of the hall staring out of the window. He didn't want to be around anyone.

"KJ?" KJ turned around and now instead of a defiant man trying to come off to the world as hard, Levi saw a scared young man. He could see that he had been crying.

"Hey, man, thanks for coming. Sorry about ruining your trip and everything."

"You didn't ruin my trip; I would have been very upset if no one had called me. So how is she doing?" KJ worked to compose himself. He was losing the battle with the tears.

"Um, the doctors—uh, they're not sure if she's going to make it. But you can pray can't you, Rev? I don't want my grandmomma to die." He gave up all pretense of not crying as his body racked with tears. Levi pulled him close to him.

"Listen, KJ, I'm going to go in. I'm going to pray the prayer of faith, but ultimately it's whatever God's will is. And we have the assurance of knowing that your grandmother is ready to meet the Lord if He decides to call her home. I'm going to ask the nurses if I can go in for a minute, then I'll come get you and we'll go downstairs and grab a soda and talk, okay?"

"Okay."

Mother Pearl had suffered a massive heart attack the night before. Levi went in and stood at the foot of her bed. Just several days ago they had talked and shared. Who would have believed that now she was fighting for her life. She opened her eyes and tried to speak. Levi walked to her bedside and took her hand.

"Don't try to talk, Mother."

"Is KJ all right?" she managed to get out.

"Yes, ma'am I just talked to him. He's worried about you, though."

"I can't leave him now, Pastor. Lord knows I can't."

"Mother, you have to concentrate on you right now. I'll take care of KJ until you come home, I promise. You rest and try not to worry. I want to pray with you and we're going to believe God that you're coming home soon. Is that all right?"

"Yes." Her voice was barely above a whisper.

"Father, in the name of Jesus I praise You right now for who You are. Lord, just on today I testified that you are a provider, a prince of peace, a victorious Lord! Father, I know that You're also a healer. Lord, even though I'm confident that if this mother of the church would leave here right now, she would be present with you, I'm asking you to leave her here with those of us who love her. Lord, I know you have a special place prepared for her, but, Father God, she's asking for some more time here on earth. She sees a need here that she wants to meet. And, Lord, we're asking for Your help in that situation, also. Even so, Lord, you know best. We want Your will to be done. Lord, we give you the praise, the glory, and the honor, in Jesus' name. Amen, and Amen. It's going to be all right, Mother." Tears were streaming down Mother Pearl's face. Levi bent and kissed her gently. "Get some rest, I'll check on you later."

Chapter 35

Levi went back to where he had left KJ. "Come on, let's go have that talk now."

For the next hour, the two men talked. Levi told him how much his grandmother was worried about leaving him. He told him that both of them wanted to see him get his life straightened out. "How did you start being a part of a gang?" Levi asked him bluntly. He knew he might never get a chance to talk so frankly with him again.

"It's not the kind of gang you're talking about where someone's always getting shot or killed. It's mostly just hanging out, you know what I'm saying, and knowing we got each others' back."

"But if you have a beef with somebody, doesn't that mean all your boys have a beef, too?"

"Something like that."

"Don't you think it's childish to be mad at somebody just because your friend is mad?"

"Naw, it's just they know if they mess with one of us, they got to mess with all of us, you know what I'm saying?"

"No, I don't know what you're saying. From where I'm sitting, I see a woman who has made sacrifices for you. And now that you're a man and able to help her out—make her golden years a little easier—you've taken to the streets. You need a job, you need to contribute to the household. That woman lying upstairs loves you. She would take a bullet for you. If you love her, you need to get your act together." KJ had turned his head. "Look, KJ, I know you're in pain, I know you're worrying about your grandmother, and I hate coming down on you like this. But if your grandmother dies tonight, she's going to live again. You've got to think about what would happen to you if you went out and got killed tonight. You don't want to spend eternity lost."

"Well, you picked a fine time to come down on me, man. I called you here to pray for my grandmother, not preach to me."

"Let me ask you this. If you saw a child about to walk in the street in front of a car and his mother was sick, would you wait until the mother was well before telling the child to watch out?"

"Man, that's lame. You know that's not the same thing."

"It's the very same thing. There's never a good time to try to help someone turn his life around, when he sees nothing wrong with his life. I'm telling you tonight that God loves you as much as he loves your grandmother. And he wants you within the ark of safety."

"I'm just not ready to get saved right now."

"I respect that. But will you come by the church sometime, so we can talk?

"You talking about on a Sunday?"

"I'm there during the week, too. Anytime you want to talk. If you don't feel comfortable talking in my office, we can get in the car and ride out somewhere."

"You're all right, man. You really are."

"I appreciate that. Let's go back upstairs and check on your grandmother."

Mother Pearl stayed in intensive care for another three days. She was then moved to a private room. The doctors said that with part-time nursing help, she could come home in a few days.

Chapter 36

That Wednesday night after Bible study, the members were standing around talking. “Oh, Pastor, and Shalan, what with everybody worrying about Mother Pearl and everything, we forgot to tell you what happened Christmas morning during service.

Some of the young people started giggling and even the older ones were smiling.

“What happened?” Levi asked.

“Guess who came to church?”

“I have no idea.”

“Your old girlfriend.”

“Vanessa?” Levi asked incredulously. He hadn’t spoken to Vanessa since last summer. After the Lamars left Maryland he had called Atlanta, wanting to say he was sorry things hadn’t worked out between them and that he hoped there were no hard feelings. She had refused to take his calls, telling her daddy to tell him not to call her again. He hadn’t.

“Yes siree. Walked in here making a grand entrance in her red suit and a hat as wide as the door.”

“Perry,” his wife cautioned, “you’re in church.”

“Okay, maybe not that wide, but it was wide.”

“Anyway, Rev. Hampton was in the pulpit sitting behind the podium so I guess she assumed it was you.” Kim, who was in charge of the video ministry that Levi had started, took up the story.

“When Mother Davis asked the visitors to stand, Jay caught my eye because we don’t usually tape that. I just nodded my head because I knew you had to see it to believe it.”

“Anyway,” Mother Ingram said, “she gets up, says she is here to visit her fiancé, the Rev. Levi Leach. And she’s sure we’re enjoying him.”

"Get out of here!" said Levi. "I know y'all are pulling my leg."

"I kid you not," Perry assured him. "Mary, am I lying?"

"No, afraid not. Pastor, you didn't tell us you had two fiancées."

"I don't. That woman is… I won't even say. So what happened?"

"Well, when Rev. Hampton got up to preach, he welcomed everyone to the service and said that he was here filling in for the pastor in his absence—that he was in North Carolina with his family attending his sister's wedding. Everyone was careful not to look over there at her."

"Yeah, we knew the camera was rolling anyway."

"I'm sorry if that was embarrassing for you," Levi told his members.

"Embarrassing? It was funny to me," one of the teenagers said.

"Well, it's embarrassing for me," Levi said. "I'm going to call her when I get home and get to the bottom of this."

"Have you talked to her at all since the revival?" asked Perry.

"No, not a word."

"Well, I would just let sleeping dogs lie. She knows that she's not your fiancée, and it's obvious that she thought that announcing herself in public as your fiancée would put you in an awkward position."

"Yeah, I guess you're right. I just can't believe the nerve of her."

"Just thank God that you saw the light before you married her."

"Yeah." He turned to Shalan who hadn't said a word the whole conversation. "Come on, I'll drop you off." She had ridden with Perry, Mary, and Mother Ingram.

"No, that's okay. I'll just ride back with them." Levi met Mother Ingram's eye. She gave a slight nod and took Kendrick's hand.

"Good night everyone," Levi said. "Shalan, would you walk out with me, please?" Not wanting to cause a scene, Shalan reluctantly followed Levi out. When he got to his car he opened the passenger side. "Get in, please."

"I told you I would ride back the way I came."

"Baby, don't punish me for something that wasn't my fault."

Shalan got in the car. Levi tried to make conversation but she gave one-syllable answers. Levi pulled in at the park. "Okay, say what's on your mind."

"Nothing's on my mind."

"You're sure?"

"Yes." He reached across the seat and tried to kiss her, but she turned her head and looked out the window. Levi sat and tapped a beat on the steering wheel. "Will you please stop that?"

"No, because at least it's got you talking."

"Maybe we're rushing into this marriage thing."

"Okay, now we're getting somewhere."

"It's obvious Vanessa wants you back."

"Go on."

"She's more your type." Levi could hear the tears threatening.

"What is my type? Oh, don't tell me, I remember, tall and light-skinned, right?"

"And pretty, don't forget pretty," Shalan said.

"Shalan, look at me, please." She continued to look out at the night. "Please."

She turned toward him but lowered her head.

"Baby, I can't rewrite the past. Even if I could I don't know if I would. Because everything that happened made us what we are. I don't know what I need to do to make you feel secure, but if I have to spend the rest of my life trying, that's just what I have to do. Shalan, I love you. I want you to look in my senior memory book the next time we go to Sanford. Do you know why?" She shook her head. "Because there's a section in there where we filled out our opinions. Where it asks for the prettiest girl in school I have your name. Even before I knew I loved you, I always thought you were the prettiest girl I knew. But I didn't fall in love with you because of that. I love what you are inside. And especially now since we both know Christ, I think you were hand picked for me by God. And I couldn't be happier about it, because I agree with God's choice. I don't know what kind of game Vanessa is playing, but it just ain't gonna work, because you are my choice. When Valentine's Day gets here, I'm going to love you all night long and that's what's up."

Shalan looked at him. "Do you really love me? You aren't just marrying me because of Kendrick."

"No, I'm not. I tried to find you before I knew anything about Kendrick. No one I asked knew where you were. I tried your college roommates, everyone. I'm marrying you because I love you."

"I love you, too. I'm sorry I acted jealous. Sometimes I just think something is going to happen and we don't get married."

"Come here." Levi kissed her hungrily. "Oh, baby, you just don't know how much I love you. If you did, you wouldn't be insecure."

"I'm working on it."

"Any time you need reassurance, you know where to call."

"Okay." He reached over and gave her another kiss.

"I need to take you home. I need a cold shower in the worst way."

Shalan laughed.

"Oh, so it's funny to you?"

"No," she answered, still laughing.

"Just remember, payback is coming."

Chapter 37

The Sunday that Mother Pearl came back to church late in January was a day of rejoicing. When Levi looked out and saw KJ with her, his eyes filled with tears. KJ had been by to see him twice since the night at the hospital. Once, they had gone to get something to eat. The other time, an unseasonably warm day, they had shot baskets outside of the church. That day, Levi had glanced up to see Jamal and Jalan pull up. When Jalan saw KJ, he pulled off. Jalan had yet to come to a service, although Jamila was there every Sunday.

Sheba had joined the choir shortly after moving in with Mother Ingram. As the choir stood to sing, she took the microphone. "As you know, the first time I came to this church, I was thinking about taking my own life. But God had other plans for me. Satan should have grabbed me when he had the chance, because now I'm sold out for Jesus. I heard a song on the radio the other day by Kurt Carr and I knew I had to learn that song because it's my testimony, church. It's like it was written just for me. Because, you see, I almost let go, but God held me close and he wouldn't let go. The song goes like this."

As she sang, Levi looked at the congregation. KJ seemed to be especially paying attention. He hoped it was the message and not the messenger he was paying attention to.

Sheba was a pretty girl. Levi knew that Billy, the guy Kara had first tried to hook Shalan up with, was interested in asking her out. Levi had asked him to give Sheba a little more time to heal before he dated her. Billy was 26 and surprisingly he and Levi had hit it off. As a matter of fact he was going to be in his wedding. Levi looked over at him now as he played the keyboards as Sheba sang. Levi stood to his feet as she got to the close of her song. "Stand on your feet, church. We have something to praise God for! Our sister that just ministered to us in song was just about to give up. The breakthrough was just ahead of her and she couldn't see it. But God held her close; He wouldn't let go. Mother Pearl is back with us! God saw fit to send her back to us. Hallelujah, that's something to give Him thanks for. You may be seated if you can. Somebody else is at the edge of a breakthrough. It's not by accident or chance that Sister Sheba sang that song today. I know it ministered to somebody in here this morning. When I feel the hand of God moving, I don't go my usual way. I don't have to preach before I give the altar call. Those of you who go here know I might give the altar call at any time during the service. If you hear God speaking to you, if you've been putting Him off, but you feel that this is your day, come on now. We're going to wait for you. Choir, sing just a little more of that song. It's speaking to somebody. If you don't come today, don't put it off much longer."

Jamila got up and started forward. "Praise the Lord." Jamal quickly got up and went with his mother down the aisle. Mother Ingram and Mother Davis embraced her as she made her way to the altar, tears streaming down her face. "What do you want from the Lord today?" Levi asked her quietly.

"I want to get saved."

"Do you believe that Jesus died for your sins? Do you believe that He rose again from the dead?"

"Yes."

"You know that He loves you and wants to come into your heart?"

"Yes."

"We've all sinned and fallen short of the glory of God, but when we confess those sins, He is faithful and just to forgive. Pray with me now."

Chapter 38

As Levi went back in the pulpit to preach a short message, he noticed that KJ had left. This made him smile on the inside. He knew the Spirit of God was dealing with him mightily. That's why he had left. Levi was confident that he would be back. He just had to be patient. It was all in God's timing.

That afternoon, he and Shalan sat at Mother Ingram's kitchen table going over final details for their wedding. Shalan was leaving for New York, Friday, for a bridal shower that LaTia and her Aunt Faye were giving her. "Now are you sure everyone has been measured for their tuxes?"

"Check."

"The flowers have been ordered… do you have the rings?"

"Oh, do we need rings?"

"Levi!"

"Just kidding. Everything is under control. Stop worrying. Isn't that Sandra's job, to do the worrying?" Sandra, one of Shalan's co-workers, was directing the wedding.

"I'm not worrying."

"What are you writing now?"

"I'm writing my wedding party down in my bridal book." There were going to be six bridesmaids: Kara, Sherise, Alisa, Pamela, Sheba, and Remika, her college roommate. Angie and LaTia were her matrons of honor. Delisa had opted to be a hostess at the reception. Mr. Leach was his son's best man. All three of his brothers were groomsmen along with Billy, Travis, and two of his frat brothers. Kendrick, of course, was the ring bearer and Mother Davis' great-granddaughter was going to be flower girl. They had decided to let some of the young people from church participate. Two of the boys were going to light the candles, and two were going to serve as ushers. A group of girls were going to sing a prayer after the vows were spoken. Aunt Faye and Mother Ingram were both going to sit on the front pew on Shalan's side of the church. Her dad's brother, Chip, and his family were coming up from South Carolina. Her Uncle Chip was going to escort her down the aisle, and Rev. McLean was coming up from North Carolina to perform the ceremony. Some of the ladies of the church had insisted on cooking for the wedding rehearsal. The church family was filled with excitement and anticipation.

Levi couldn't believe that in less than three weeks, he would be a married man; he couldn't wait. He had seen Vanessa's number on his caller ID once since her surprise Christmas visit, but since she hadn't left a message, he hadn't returned the call. Now he wondered if maybe he should have. What if she stormed in during the wedding? Oh well, he had told Shalan to stop worrying, now he was doing the same thing.

"Penny for your thoughts?" Shalan broke in.

"Oh, nothing." She gave him a knowing look.

"I was just imagining what would happen if Vanessa walked in on our wedding."

"I would probably forget I was saved," Shalan said only half joking.

"Oh, so you would handle things?" Levi teased.

"Without a doubt." Levi shook his head. He knew Shalan couldn't hurt a fly even before she was saved.

Chapter 39

The Saturday that Shalan was gone Levi was on his way to his car when he saw Jalan and Jamal pull up in front of his house. "What's up?"

"Nothing. Just came by to check you out. Jamal says he's in your wedding."

"Yeah, he's lighting the candles. Why?"

"I just didn't believe him, that's all."

"Are you coming to the wedding?"

"I didn't know I was invited."

"Everyone's invited."

"I don't know, man, I don't have that many church clothes."

"Well, just come clean. All eyes are going to be on my beautiful bride anyway."

"Yeah, she's fine all right."

"Watch out there, now." The boys laughed.

"Well we're not gonna hold you up, man, I can see you're about to roll out."

"Come on, you can ride with me."

"Where you going?"

"To the rest home to do some visiting." Jamal moved toward the car, but Jalan held back.

"Naw, I don't think so."

"Come on, it'll do you good to think about somebody besides yourself sometimes. And come to think of it, I haven't seen you in church, yet."

"I was coming one Sunday, but I heard you were out of town."

"How convenient. Come on; get in the car. I might buy you a burger on the way back." Although Jalan grumbled, Levi could tell he wasn't as reluctant to go as he pretended to be. "So, Jalan, are you still running with that gang?"

"Why does everyone insist I'm in a gang? Where did that come from?"

"I don't know. Tell me."

"It's more like a club. It's not like a gang where they kill you if you try to get out." Levi glanced at him. "Why, is that what you heard?"

"Something like that."

"Somebody's been watching too much TV."

"So what kinds of things does this club do?"

"We just hang out."

"Just hang out, huh?"

"Yeah, what's wrong with that?" Levi was silent, trying to decide how far to push. Jalan repeated his question. "What's wrong with that?"

"Okay, what's wrong with that is you're 18. You didn't graduate from high school. You're not working. You're still living at home. What are your future plans, what goals have you set for yourself?"

"At least I'm just 18. You ought to be talking to your boy, KJ. He's 20 living at home with his grandmother."

"So that's your defense? When you don't have an answer just try to turn the focus on someone else?"

"Man, take me back to get my car."

"So when we talk man-to-man and you don't like what I say, you're always going to run?"

"I just got better things to do."

"Okay, I'll take you to get your car when we leave the nursing home." Jamal had sat up tensely in the back seat. Now he leaned back and relaxed. Levi could hold his own with his brother. And as much as Jalan tried to deny it, Jamal was sure he felt special just as he did knowing that someone besides their mother cared about them.

"You know, I've been thinking about talking to someone at the community college to see if we could have a GED program at the church. Would you come to it?"

"I might."

"Jamal, remind me one day next week to look into that."

"Okay, Pastor."

The afternoon spent at the nursing home couldn't have gone better if Levi had written the script. Jalan and Jamal played checkers and card games with some of the residents in the recreation hall while he visited with some of the bedridden patients. He had audiotapes of Sunday's service to hand out to those who wanted them. When he went to collect the boys they chastised him for not staying long. Levi smiled and glanced at the clock on the wall. Both boys were surprised to see they had been there for over two hours.

Levi told Shalan about his day later on the phone. They talked about the possibility of getting Jamal to talk to other young people in the church about a nursing home ministry. "If they could send over two or three people a week, it would give the residents something to look forward to every week and not just every now and then." The conversation then became more personal. "I sure do miss you, baby."

"I miss you, too."

"So how was your shower?"

"Oh we had a lot of fun. I got a lot of nice things."

"Did you get anything special to wear on the honeymoon?"

"You are sooo bad."

"I'll accept that. Did you?"

"Maybe, maybe not. You'll just have to wait and see."

"Okay, I like surprises. What's my son doing?"

"He's about asleep. He didn't take a nap today."

"Kiss him good night for me, and tell him his daddy loves him."

"I will. Does his daddy love his mommy, too?"

"He sure does, with all his heart. Call me before you get on the highway tomorrow."

"I will. Love you."

Finally, the week of the wedding had come. Levi's family came in the day before rehearsal. Shalan and Angie went shopping together to get some things for her to take on her two-day honeymoon. LaTia, Aunt Faye, and Alisa were expected to arrive later tonight as was Uncle Chip. Tyrese wasn't coming until the night before the wedding. The bridesmaids and matrons of honor were going to spend the night at Mother Ingram's tonight. Tomorrow would be rehearsal and the dinner afterward and the next day Shalan would be Mrs. Levi Leach.

Chapter 40

The Leach men were leaving the manse on their way to the rehearsal. The women had gone on ahead. Just as they were about to get in two vehicles, they saw KJ coming up the sidewalk. "Make it quick, son," Will Leach told Levi.

"I'll just be a minute," Levi told his dad and his brothers. "Hey, man, what's up?" he greeted KJ.

"I need to talk to you."

"Can it wait? I'm on my way to my wedding rehearsal."

KJ looked crestfallen. "Yeah, I guess so." As they stood in the driveway they saw Jalan's car coming. He slowed down, and then speeded up when he saw KJ and Levi. KJ's eyes followed the car down the street.

"What's up with you two anyway?" Levi asked. "Don't you think this rivalry has gone on long enough?"

"I'm willing to squash it. He accused me of stealing his shoes out of the gym back in junior high. I was in the 9th grade, and I had P.E. right after his class."

"So why did he think you did it?"

"'Cause that next week I came to school with some Jordans on. But my dad had sent them to me. I got called to the office and everything, man. But my shoes were two sizes bigger than his. Since then I just haven't had any use for him. Plus his boy, Tony, pulled a gun on me one night for dancing with his old lady. And that was so funny to Jalan."

"Well you two are men now. And you aren't in the Wild West; y'all need to stop carrying these guns around. Don't look at me like that, I know you have one, too."

Mr. Leach gently tapped his horn. Levi glanced at his watch.

"Listen, I have to go, are you sure you don't want to tell me what's on your mind?"

"You go on, I'll talk to you next week sometime."

"You're sure? What's it about?"

"I want to be saved, Pastor."

He had never called Levi "pastor" before; he usually addressed him as "man."

"Does it have to be on a Sunday?"

"No, of course not, Jesus will save you today. Come on in." Levi signaled for everyone else to go ahead. "I'll only be a few minutes," he promised.

"Don't let me have to come get you, boy," Hugh told him.

Levi looked around. "I don't see a boy. Where is he?"

"You'll find out if I have to come looking for you."

"You won't. I don't want to make Shalan mad the day before the wedding."

He and KJ went inside and, after explaining to him God's plan for salvation, Levi patiently answered all of KJ's questions. KJ invited Jesus to be his personal savior.

Levi stood and embraced him as they both cried. After talking for a few minutes, Levi said, "This is the best wedding present you could ever give me, KJ. Are you going to be at the wedding tomorrow?"

"Yeah, if you want me to."

"Of course I want you to. As a matter of fact, why don't you come over to the church with me now? They've got enough food to feed an army. And you talking about some women that can cook! Man, I can't even tell you, you just have to come see."

"You sure they won't care?"

"Man, come on here. I'll let you tell your own news, though when you're ready. I won't mention it."

Levi had parked his car on the street earlier in the day since so many vehicles were in the driveway. The two men started down the sidewalk, talking and laughing. All at once gunshots were fired. A bullet went right by KJ's head, too close for comfort. He hit the ground sweating despite the cold day. Minutes later all was quiet.

"Man, that was close," he said to Levi as he cautiously looked around before getting up. When Levi didn't answer him he looked around. Pastor Levi Leach lay in his own blood the day before his wedding.

Chapter 41

"Oh my God, no!" KJ shouted. "Please, somebody help me!" He didn't see a single soul on the street. He reached for his cell phone and dialed 911. "Please, I need an ambulance right away to 716 Magnolia Street. Please hurry."

"What is your emergency?"

"My pastor's been shot. He's not moving!"

"And your name?"

"KJ Finch. Please stop asking questions and just hurry!"

"Someone is on the way. Is he conscious?"

"No, he looks like he's dead."

"Do you know CPR?"

"NO. Please just tell me what to do! Hold up, I see a police car coming."

"Okay, let the officer assist you. The ambulance should be there shortly."

The officer didn't say much to KJ; he checked Levi to see if he was breathing. He was breathing, but barely.

"He's bleeding awfully bad," KJ observed, his voice thick with tears. He took his shirt off and handed it to the officer who tried to slow the bleeding down. He checked his pulse.

"Go to the street and watch for the ambulance. Make sure they don't miss the house. We're losing him." He then started CPR.

Chapter 42

"Well, I believe your brother changed his mind about getting married." Shalan tried to joke, but in reality she was getting worried.

"You know how Levi is. He can't turn away from other people's problems. Still he needs to get his butt on over here. People have things to do."

"Yeah, like eat that food I smell." Rod got in the conversation.

"You boys go see what's holding him up," their mother told them.

"Better not send all three. Keep one of them here for ransom. Send two, that way they can pick him up and throw him in the car," Mr. Leach joked. Everyone was in a festive mood. They had rehearsed everything they could without the groom being present. Now they just needed him for a few minutes, then they could finish up and eat the delicious food everyone had smelled for the past hour.

Greg and Rod got in their dad's car and started back to the manse, singing with the radio. They had to pull over just before they turned onto Magnolia Street, to let an ambulance go by. "I hate to see them with the lights flashing because you always wonder about the person inside, whether they'll make it to the hospital in time," Rod said. He had always been the most sensitive of all the boys. As he spoke the words, Greg felt a strange feeling come over him. So much so, that he stepped on the accelerator. When they got near the house they could see police cars in front of it, and curious onlookers lining the sidewalks.

Greg pulled up to the curb and the two brothers jumped out of the car. KJ was standing, talking to a female officer who was taking notes. He had a jacket thrown over his shoulders, but they could see he was shirtless.

"What's going on here, officer?" Greg asked the nearest police officer.

"Could I see some ID, it's just routine."

Greg was speaking even as he went for his wallet. "I'm Greg Leach, and this is my brother, Rod. Please, has something happened to my brother? He lives here."

"Yes, I'm sorry to tell you, but there was a drive-by shooting. Your brother was shot."

"Is he okay?" Rod asked.

"One of the officers did CPR on him before the ambulance got here. He's alive, but from what I've been told, he might not make it to the hospital. Does he have other family that you need to notify?"

"Yes, they're all at his church at his wedding rehearsal, waiting for him." Rod and Greg were trying to absorb all that was being said, but they knew they were going to soon lose it. This was their beloved brother the cop was talking about. The officer whistled softly.

"That's a bummer. I'm so sorry. You guys need to notify the other family members."

"Can you tell us how to get to the hospital? We're not from here."

"Come on, I'll give you a police escort to the hospital. Better yet, just get in with me. I'll have an officer follow in your car." KJ noticed them leaving and ran over. He was still crying.

"Can I come with you?"

"Yes, get in." KJ and Rod got in the back while Greg jumped in the front seat with the policeman, hurriedly tossing the keys to the woman who had been questioning KJ. Rod took his cell phone out. He had Christ's Church programmed. When someone came on the line he asked to speak with Travis Ingram.

"Travis, this is Rod, Levi's brother."

"Hey, man, what's holding you guys up?"

"Travis," Rod's voice broke.

"What's wrong?"

"Levi was shot in a drive-by shooting. He might not make it, man."

"Jesus."

"I need you to tell my family and Shalan and get them to the hospital as soon as possible."

"Okay, where are they taking him?" After asking the officer, Rod told him.

"And Travis?"

"Yeah, man."

"Please pray."

"Oh, no doubt, man, no doubt."

Chapter 43

Travis rushed back to the sanctuary. He motioned for Kara to come to him. "Go sit beside Shalan and have one of the other ladies sit beside Mrs. Leach. Have someone take the kids downstairs."

"What's wrong?"

"Just do it, babe. I'll tell everybody at one time." Kara moved swiftly, despite her pregnancy. "Listen up, everybody. There's no easy way to say this. Pastor Levi has been shot. He's in critical condition, and we need to get to the hospital right away."

Wails and moans rang out. Shalan, Angie, and Pamela took it especially hard, but Mrs. Leach remained dry-eyed.

"Where is my baby? Take me to him."

"Come on, I'll drive you. Kara, please let everyone downstairs know what's going on, and get hold of Dad. Then come on to the hospital. Okay, honey?"

"Okay."

Rod and Greg got up to embrace their parents and Shalan as soon as they arrived.

"I want to see him!" Shalan cried.

"The doctors are in with him now."

"Have you seen him?"

"No, when we were going to the house we met the ambulance. KJ was with him when it happened." Mr. Leach glanced over at KJ.

"Did he see who did it?"

"No, but he told the officer that Jalan, Jamal's brother," he looked toward Jamal, "had ridden by the house about a half hour earlier. He thinks maybe Jalan was shooting at him and shot Levi instead."

"I don't believe that," Shalan declared. "All these years they've been hating each other, why would he try to kill him in front of Levi? That doesn't make sense."

"Anyway, they're looking for Jalan just to question him."

A nurse came out and asked to see Levi's immediate family. She looked surprised at the number of people in the waiting area. The family was taken to a room. "We've been trying to get him stable enough to do surgery," a doctor informed them. "We're going to need someone, next of kin, to sign a consent form."

"Can we see him?" his mother questioned.

"Not at this time. We'll try to let you see him briefly before we take him to surgery." As the word spread, more of the church members arrived, Jamila among them.

"KJ, I heard you said my son did this. Are you sure?"

"What!" Jamal cried out. This was the first he had heard of it. "If he shot Pastor Levi, he's no more a brother of mine."

"I didn't say he did it. I just told the officer he passed by the house, and that he didn't like me."

"Well that's as good as saying he did it!" Jamila cried angrily.

"Please," Rev. McLean intervened, "the family does not need this right now. What they need is our prayers. I know you're upset. But if your son is innocent, I'm sure the police will find that out. But right now, a young man that I love is fighting for his life. We don't need this right now."

"I'm sorry," apologized Jamila. "My boys love Pastor Levi. I just can't believe that Jalan would do something like this."

"Let's join hands and pray," Rev. McLean told the group.

"It's so many of us, maybe we need to go outside," someone suggested.

"No, I want to be here in case the doctor comes out," Shalan said. The group joined hands and started praying. Shalan went and stood in the hall, away from everyone else after the prayer. "Please, God, don't take him from me. Where's my son?" she asked when she went back in the room.

"He's still at the church."

"I want him with me; I need to tell him what's going on."

"Are you sure that's a good idea?" one of the ladies asked.

"Yes, I want him here. Just for a little while. Then will you take him home, LaTia?"

"I want to stay here with you. I'll call Tyrese and have him come get him when you think he's getting too tired."

"Thank you, Tia. I love you."

"I love you, too." The doctor came out shortly after that and said they were about to take Levi to surgery.

"Very quickly, we're going to let the immediate family go in just for a minute."

"Has he regained consciousness at all?" Hugh asked.

"No, and I must warn you, he looks bad. So please, if you think you're going to get hysterical, don't go in. We're not sure how much he can hear at this point."

The doctor's words still did not prepare them. This couldn't be their beloved Levi lying there as if he were dead. After what seemed only a moment, they were asked to step out of the room.

Perry had gotten there by the time they came out. He encouraged some of the people to go wait for word at the church. Mother Davis, Mother Ingram and Mother Pearl came by. Perry suggested they all go spend the night at his mother's house. He promised them that he would call as soon as they knew anything. Shalan insisted that her bridesmaids go back to the church to eat. They were reluctant to leave her. She got them to go only by asking them to bring her and the other family members some food. She knew that she wouldn't be able to eat a bite and they knew it, too. When Kendrick got there she took him in the chapel and explained to him gently that his daddy had been shot and that they were praying that he would be better soon. "If he doesn't get better, is he going to go see your momma and daddy?"

"Yes, baby. But let's pray he decides to come see us instead. Okay?"

"Okay, Mommy. Should we pray that he gets better before my birthday?"

"Yes, that's a good idea." She kissed him on the cheek and held him close.

"Let's pray right now, Mommy." Together the two of them knelt at the altar where people of all faiths and all walks of life had prayed for years.

Chapter 44

A few minutes after they returned to the waiting room, they saw Jalan come in. You could feel the tenseness in the room. Jamal broke down in tears as soon as he saw him. "Jamal, I swear on everything that's holy, I did not shoot Pastor Levi. I love him, you know that." He was crying, too. "If you don't believe me, call the police station. I had to go down there to see if any gunpowder was on my hands. It wasn't."

Jamal went over and hugged him.

"I believe you, man."

"We all do," Shalan told him. "You're welcome to sit with us for a while if you want to."

"Pastor Levi invited me to the wedding," Jalan explained, "I had gone to the mall to get an outfit to wear. I was on my way over there to show him. But he had company so I just kept going."

"I have something to say," KJ said. "Jalan, I'm sorry I thought of you first thing. If I hadn't held him up, he would have been at the church and not gotten shot. It's all my fault."

"No one's blaming you, son," Mr. Leach told him. "We need to blame whoever did this."

"The reason I had gone by," KJ continued, "I wanted to get saved, and I did." There was a chorus of "Praise the Lord" from everyone in the room. "The first thing Pastor Levi wanted me to do was talk to you, Jalan, and see if we can come to an understanding. He said he loves us both and it hurts him to see us act like we've been acting. So, man, I'm sorry for today and for everything I've done wrong to you over the years."

"Do you accept his apology?" Perry asked.

"Yeah. Hey, man, I'm sorry, too, for, you know, everything." He walked over to KJ and gave him a brotherly hug, both of them still in tears. "Is he going to be all right, man?" Jalan asked.

"We don't know, man, we just don't know." After what seemed like forever a doctor came in the room and asked to speak to the Leach family. "We're all family here," Mrs. Leach told him. "You can speak freely."

"We've finished the surgery. As a doctor, I have to tell you, it doesn't look good. We actually lost him on the operating table. His heart stopped beating, but we were able to bring him back. He's breathing with the help of a respirator, and if he holds on until tomorrow, I'll be a little more hopeful, but right now, I would be very surprised if he makes it through the night. That's what I'm obligated to tell you as a doctor. But I'm a Christian. And as a Christian, I'm telling you to tell the Devil he's a liar. I would send so many prayers up to Heaven that God himself would say, 'Enough, already.' I never met your son, but some of the nurses recognized him and said what a true man of God he is. I just don't think God is going to call him home right now. Be encouraged."

"Thank you, doctor. We appreciate everything you've done."

Perry called the church to give them an update. He wanted to get a round-the-clock prayer vigil started. "Leave the church open all night," he instructed. "We want at least two people laying at the altar before God every hour on the hour. I'll be here all night doing the same thing with the people here." He called his mother's next to tell them what the doctor had said. Over in the night Tyrese came and took a sleeping Kendrick out of his mother's weary arms.

Hours after Levi's surgery, the doctors let the family go in two at a time to see him. They had asked if it were all right to say something to him. "Sure, at this point it won't hurt and it might help." When Shalan went in she told him he was not going to get out of marrying her that easily.

"I love you, Levi," she told him, trying to keep her voice steady. She looked for any sign, no matter how slight, that he had heard her. The only noise in the room was the rhythm of the respirator.

Chapter 45

Early the next morning a detective came to the hospital. "Do you know if Mr. Leach has any enemies in Georgia?"

"Not that we know of," they answered almost in unison.

"We're just following all leads. A car with a Georgia license plate was clocked yesterday going 55 in a residential area over near your son's house. The officer wrote a ticket to," he looked at his clipboard, "Milton Watson. Name ring a bell?"

"No. I'm afraid I'm not following you. What does his getting a ticket have to do with Levi getting shot?" Mr. Leach asked.

"Maybe nothing. One of Mr. Leach's, er Rev. Leach's neighbors reported that a car of the same make with a Georgia license plate was seen on that street several times yesterday. The witness, who's recovering from surgery, said he seemed to be watching the house. He was asleep when the actual shooting took place so he doesn't know if the car was in the area at that time. But the ticket was written right before the shooting."

"If he did it, he could be back in Georgia by now," Angie lamented.

"That's true. But you're forgetting, we have a name and home address. The man must not be too bright."

"Levi went to seminary in Georgia, but I can't imagine anyone he made mad enough to come to Maryland to kill him after all of this time."

"We're just covering all our bases. We're also exploring the possibility that the shooter was going for the other young man and missed his target. But in that case he would have had to be tailing him since Kendrick doesn't visit Mr. Leach on a regular basis. He doesn't recall anyone following him. He's pretty streetwise so he notices things like that." They sat in silence for a minute. "What part of

Georgia was the seminary?"

"Atlanta."

"My hunch is telling me there's a connection. That's where Watson is from."

Shalan had been listening to the exchange, not contributing anything.

"You don't suppose…" Her voice trailed off.

"What?" The detective pounced on it. "Anything that comes to mind even if you don't think it's significant might help us. The more days that pass, the harder it's going to be to get at the truth."

"Levi dated a girl in Atlanta. She came up here recently and told everyone at our church she was his fiancée. Everyone knew that was a lie because he was engaged to me at the time and hadn't seen her in months."

"Interesting. What's her name?"

"Vanessa Lamar?"

"Vanessa Lamar, Vanessa Lamar. For some reason that name rings a bell." He turned to another detective who had come in the room after the conversation started. "Fred, why is the name Lamar ringing a bell?"

"Did her father pastor a big church up this way at one time?" Fred asked.

"Yeah, I believe Levi found that out just before they broke up," Mrs. Leach said.

"If my memory serves me correctly—I'll have to check the files when I go back—she got violent with a boyfriend back when she was in high school. Her father paid the guy off to drop the charges. Shortly after that the family moved. If it's the same family, she could very well be involved. Her father used to buy her way out of a lot of trouble."

"I think we need to see if Mr. Watson is still in the area, and if not I'll call the police department in Atlanta, have them go by and see if he's back down there."

All throughout the day, the family kept a vigil at the hospital. They took turns going over to Mother Ingram's where food had been sent over, getting a bite to eat, grabbing a quick shower, and rushing back to the hospital. At 5:00 everyone's thoughts took the same direction, this was the time Levi should have been saying his vows instead of lying in a hospital bed hooked up to a machine with all kinds of tubes. Angie jumped up in frustration and began to sob uncontrollably. "If I find out she had anything to do with this, I'll kill her, I swear I will!" Her husband got up and took her in his arms.

"Shh, baby. It's going to be all right."

"It's not fair. It's not fair. My brother hasn't hurt anybody. He's always trying to help everybody. Oh, God, why? Why my brother? Please, God, don't let him die."

Everyone in the room was crying with her. Shalan got up and went over to them, and the three of them embraced.

"Angie, no matter what happens, I will always consider you my sister-in-law as well as a sister. I will never love another man the way I love Levi. But we can't give up hope yet. We've got to keep believing." Angie nodded her head.

"I'm going to go in and see him, tell him to keep fighting."

"Okay. I'm going to go call and check on Kendrick."

Chapter 46

Around two the next morning, a nurse came and gently shook Shalan awake. "Come with me, please." Shalan quickly jumped up and followed her down the hallway. *Oh, no*, she thought, *she must want me to tell him goodbye*. Then she chastised herself for thinking negatively. They tiptoed in Levi's room. He was still hooked up to everything as the day before. As Shalan went closer she saw that his eyes were open. "Oh, baby, you're awake." Levi looked at her, unable to say anything. He tried to lift his arm.

"Take his hand," the nurse encouraged. Shalan took his hand and he gave a slight squeeze.

"Can you hear me, honey?" He gave a slight nod that she would have missed if she hadn't been looking so hard for it. "I love you, Levi." Another squeeze, another nod. Then off to dreamland he went. "Thank you," Shalan told the nurse. "I need to tell everyone else."

"I knew your face would be the first one he wanted to see," the nurse told her. "Just tell the others to let him get as much rest as possible today. I think the Lord is on your side on this one. You'll have to tell me more about your faith someday."

"I'll do that," Shalan promised. "Real soon." Then she rushed off to share the good news with the rest of the family.

Chapter 47

Two days later, the family and three other children celebrated Kendrick's fourth birthday. Levi was still in the ICU, but he was breathing on his own. The detectives had questioned Milton Watson and did a little embellishing. They told them they had a witness that saw him fire the shots that wounded Levi. He confessed that his distant cousin, Vanessa Lamar, had given him $500 to kill Levi. "My son's life was worth a measly $500," Mr. Leach said angrily when he heard the news.

"Apparently Watson has a coke habit and he was probably thinking in terms of how much that would buy."

"Not very much," Fred observed. "Anyway, where he's going, he'll have a little more trouble buying it. We also found out that Vanessa rode up here with him. Watson taped a conversation the two of them had. Apparently he was going to try to blackmail her when he needed more money. On the tape she doesn't come right out and say what she wants done, but with the other evidence we have, the inference is there. We're subpoenaing her bank records to show that she withdrew $500 the day of the shooting. I don't think her dad's going to buy her out of this one."

"Did she say why?" asked Mrs. Leach.

"Apparently, when she was here before she found out Levi was getting married. She saw a newspaper or something. Anyway she told Watson that Levi must have been cheating on her all along to be engaged that quickly."

"The bottom line," Fred added, "she's had issues for years and her parents always looked the other way. Anyway, I'm glad your son pulled through and I hope he gets to walk down that aisle pretty soon."

"Thank you both for everything."

"No problem. Just doing our jobs."

Shalan sat quietly beside Levi's bed, watching him sleep. He had been moved to a regular room earlier in the day, and someone from the family was staying with him at all times to make sure visitors didn't wear him out or say anything to upset him. They had agreed not to tell him about Vanessa's plot to have him killed until he was much stronger. He opened his eyes and smiled at Shalan. "Hi, sweetheart," he said in a voice still hoarse from the respirator.

"Hi, darling. Feeling better?"

"Yeah. Did they find out who did this?"

"Don't worry about that now, baby. Just get well."

"They did, didn't they?"

"All I know is that they're following some leads."

"You never were a good liar. Don't worry about it." He seemed to doze for a minute then he opened his eyes again. "Sanders Leach," he said drowsily.

"What, honey? Oh, you're asking if I want to hyphenate my name?"

"No. Kendrick. Kendrick's name. Want Kendrick to have my name." Before Shalan could agree, he was out like a light. She made a mental note to get the ball rolling on that as soon as possible.

Chapter 48

The first Sunday that Levi returned to Christ's Church was a very emotional day for him, his family, and the congregation. His parents had taken leaves of absence from their jobs to help him convalesce at home. Shalan had extended her planned vacation time. Levi sat in the congregation with his family while Perry brought the morning message. Before church dismissed Perry asked him if he wanted to have words.

Levi made his way slowly to the front, and Perry handed him the cordless microphone.

He took a deep breath trying to keep his tears at bay. "First of all I want to thank God and then I want to thank Him again. You all know more about how far he brought me from than even I do because you saw me on what could have been my deathbed. I heard about how y'all worried God on my behalf." Some people chuckled. "But seriously, I appreciate everything that was done. I appreciate how you stepped in and made sure my family had what they needed. You know, when I was lying there halfway between consciousness, I had a dream or a vision if you will. I was in a small room that was like a jail cell and it was crowded with guys my age and younger. We started talking as brothers will do and they told me they had all been shot down and killed at very young ages. One guy looked at me and said, 'We died because of our lifestyle, but, man, you need to go back. It's not your time.' And I lay there and I asked God: 'God, what does this mean?' The Holy Spirit began to speak to me. He said the room was not small, it was crowded. It was crowded because too many young people are dying senselessly, and the church..." Levi stopped talking and looked up toward Heaven, tears running freely down his face. "The church," he continued, "is in a comfort zone. Sure we talk about the problems, but we haven't addressed the problems. Too many Christians are scared to do battle with Satan. Saints, Satan has some of our young people in a stronghold and the church has been too afraid to snatch them back. You don't have to go far. I usually get here early, but today, coming in when I did, I saw young boys standing on the corners making drug deals. I saw young girls willing to sell their bodies so they can snort some cocaine before the day is over. Saints, we've been praying, but now it's time to do. Two Sundays from now, we're taking it to the streets. We're going to meet here at 10:00 for prayer, but we're having church outside. If they won't come to us, we're going to them.

Women, I'm asking you to have lemonade and tea and anything else you want to serve ready for after the service. If I were in Sanford, I'd ask Mr. Knotts to let me borrow a tent and some chairs. He's the undertaker down there. I haven't done any funerals since I've been here, praise God, so I don't know the undertakers. But if anyone knows where we can borrow chairs from, let me know. If not, we might have to buy some. I'm going to take my seat now; I don't want to prolong the service, but I'll be in my office for a while Tuesday afternoon. Please come by if you have any ideas or any concerns you want to share. God bless you."

Chapter 49

True to his word, Levi held church outside two Sundays later. The local paper had gotten wind of what Christ's Church planned to do and had given it coverage on the front page. They also ran Levi's picture and told about the drive-by shooting and the fact that it was a miracle Levi was even alive. Shalan looked out at the cool, but not cold, March morning after the church had prayed. "Levi," she motioned him over to the window, "there's a camera crew out there." Levi and some of the others came to look out.

"Good."

"Did you call them?"

"No, but we're going to have service like they aren't there. No showboating, just what the Holy Spirit leads."

"Amen, Pastor." The response from the community had been overwhelming when the article had run in the paper. Some of the local businesses had donated coffee and doughnuts. Some had given monetary gifts. Nelson Funeral Home had let them borrow chairs and two tents. The men had carried the folding chairs out of the church fellowship hall as well. At 10:55, Levi and those who had been praying with him walked over to the vacant lot where the service was going to be held. All of the seats were taken and many people were standing around. Others who were undecided about coming, but were curious nonetheless, were standing on the sidewalk within hearing distance.

The praise and worship team opened up the service. Sheba sang her testimony again.

Shalan led them in, "Because of Who You Are." They had decided to keep the beginning of the service short so that people wouldn't be tired before the sermon was preached. Levi stood and greeted the crowd and introduced himself to those who didn't know him. He opened his Bible to Luke 16 and began to read about the rich man who wanted someone to rise from the dead to warn his brothers before it was too late. He told of his recent hospital stay and how he was not going to be able to rest until he gave this message that God had been dealing with him about for almost a month.

"Some of you go the way you do because that's the only way you know. But I came to tell you today of a more excellent way." When he had finished preaching the message of salvation, Levi extended an invitation to anyone who wanted to be saved. "The choir is going to give us a number and I want everyone to just bow your heads and think about your own individual situation. If death came for you tonight, where would you spend eternity? I know the Devil has you thinking you don't want to give up the lifestyle you're living, but if you're honest with yourself, you're tired of doing what you're doing. You want to change, but you don't know if you're worthy. All of us were born in sin, shaped in iniquity. Even those of us who are in church every Sunday sometimes sin and fall short of the glory of God, but God wants you to trust Him. Invite Him into your heart today. You aren't going to suddenly become perfect, but you're going to have a friend in Jesus. Jesus will stick closer than any brother. I have three brothers, but when I have sleepless nights, it's Jesus I turn to. I never thought I would be where I am today. This is not what I would have chosen to do with my life, but God had other plans for me. When you trust him, you trust him to do what He thinks is best for you. Have you thought about it? Won't you come now? Don't look around to see who else is coming. This is a decision that only you can make. I wouldn't put it off too long. Jesus said, 'The day you hear my voice, harden not your heart.'" Levi walked down from the makeshift pulpit.

"The prison doors have been opened, what are you doing inside?" Billy immediately began to play the song. Levi started to sing. *"The prison doors have been open what are you doing inside? He made a way from earth to glory. Now he will wipe your weeping eyes."* The choir joined in. Jamal came down the aisle with one of his friends and whispered in Levi's ear that his friend wanted to be saved. Now that the first person had come forward, many followed. Some said they weren't ready to be saved, but asked Levi to pray for them. Twenty young people and 10 middle-aged people were saved that day. A white man who looked to be in his early 30s wept openly when Levi prayed with him. After everyone had gone back to his seat, he asked if he could say something.

"Sure." Levi handed him the microphone.

"Reverend, you don't know me, but I was the officer who did CPR on you the day you got shot." There was a loud burst of applause and rejoicing. The man waited for the crowd to quiet down before he continued. "I had to go home to New Hampshire the next day; my Mom was having surgery. But before my flight left, I went by the hospital to see if you had made it through the night. There were so many people there praying for you—young people, old people. I wondered what kind of man is this that all of these people care so much about him. I went in and just kind of mingled in with the crowd, not telling anyone who I was. The young man that was with you that day looked up and recognized me, but I shook my head at him. He probably thought I was there investigating, but I was just, I really don't know what made me go there. Anyway, when I came back to work I asked if they had made an arrest on the guy who murdered the preacher. Everyone was asking what preacher got murdered. I was like, you know, over on Magnolia Street. They told me you had gone home and I was speechless. When I saw the newspaper article, I knew I wanted to be here today to see for myself. If God can work miracles like this, I want him in my life, too."

Levi went over and embraced him in a brotherly hug. "Thank you, brother, for sharing that story. Thank you for acting so quickly that day. God is good, y'all. I've been to the police station looking for this man and he wasn't there. Now here he is. Because of him, my life was saved. And now because of me, his life is saved. Yet it's not us, but it's God working through us. He uses us to do his bidding, but He gets the glory!

Chapter 50

April 16th

It was Shalan's 25th birthday and her wedding day. She woke up knowing that this was going to be a blessed day. Who cared if people didn't usually wear red for April weddings? This was her wedding and red was her favorite color. Besides, she couldn't very well ask her bridesmaids to buy more dresses, now could she? Kara was going to wear a pretty red maternity dress. As big as she was getting these days she had joked with Shalan that she hoped she didn't go into early labor during the wedding.

Donna, who had been her mother's cosmetologist and friend for years, had come up from North Carolina to do Shalan's hair. "You don't have to do that," Shalan had told her when she phoned earlier in the month.

"I want to. I know your mother would insist that you be the prettiest bride ever and I'm coming up there to make sure of it." After Donna had finished with her hair and makeup, Shalan put on the lovely wedding gown that had been waiting patiently in the hall closet for months. LaTia came into the room just as she finished getting dressed.

"Oh, Tia, you look beautiful!" she exclaimed. "Red really looks good on you. Do you think I look okay?"

"Come here," LaTia ordered. She marched Shalan over to the full-length mirror. Together the cousins stood looking at their reflections. "Tell me what you see." Shalan looked at the two of them.

"Me in a white wedding dress, you in a red gown. Why? What am I supposed to see?" Donna walked up behind them.

"She wants you to see how beautiful *you* look, Shalan. Sure, Tia looks beautiful. But, you, my dear, are especially beautiful today. I know Nancy would be so proud of you." Sandra agreed with her.

"Cous, you are so modest. I guess I have enough vanity for both of us. I guess God made you humble so you could be a preacher's wife, and me vain so I could be a model." When no one made a comment, LaTia exclaimed, "Hey, I was joking, I'm not vain." There was a knock on the door.

"Come in," Shalan called.

"No, wait!" LaTia called out. "You need to see who it is first, it might be Levi."

She went and peeped out, then opened the door for her mother and Shalan's uncle.

"Oh, sweetheart, you look gorgeous. I would give anything if George were here to do the honors, but thank you for thinking enough of me to ask me to stand in for him," Uncle Chip told her. He gave her a quick kiss on the forehead. "I don't want to mess up your makeup," he told her. He stepped back so that her Aunt Faye could scrutinize her.

Her eyes began to mist.

"You look so much like Nancy did on her wedding day."

"And like I did, only a foot shorter," LaTia joked to lighten the mood. They all laughed.

Levi stood in front of the church where he usually preached, and awaited his bride. *Thank you, Jesus,* he prayed within. *Help me to always treat Shalan with love and respect.*" He smiled as his son came up the aisle with a tiny pillow in his hand, taking his part in the ceremony seriously. Minutes later he looked up and saw Shalan on her uncle's arm, coming toward him. The sight of her took his breath away. He was supposed to take her hand when she reached him, but he reached out and gave her a hug instead. The two of them embraced as the entire wedding party tried to keep from crying. Finally the two of them turned toward Rev. McLean, ready to repeat the vows that would make them husband and wife.

Levi planned to sing "Security" to Shalan after they said their vows as a surprise for her. The only problem was Shalan planned to sing "Only God Could Love You More" after they said their vows as a surprise for him. "How are we going to handle this?" the musician had asked Rev. McLean after rehearsal. "Which song do I play?" Rev. McLean told him to play Shalan's song first and he would say something to let Levi know to wait. The ceremony turned out beautifully. It was especially touching when they sang to one another because everyone present knew how close they had come to losing Levi.

Levi and Shalan had requested the deejay to play "You Are My Friend" by Patti LaBelle when they came into the reception hall. Although Patti was talking to her son in the song, it had special meaning to Levi and Shalan as a couple because they had been friends practically all of their lives. When they stood at the door, about to make an entrance, they were surprised to look up and see Patti in the flesh. The photographer caught the look of surprise on both of their faces. Later they learned that the youth department had written a letter to Ms. LaBelle, telling her how their pastor had gotten shot the day before what would have been his wedding. They told her of all the good things he had done and asked her how much she would charge them to come sing at his wedding. The letter had touched her so much that she agreed to come. Sheba and Billy sang "Spend My Life With You" by Eric Benet and Tamia for the bridal couple, and the dance team performed in their honor.

Finally the festivities began to wind down. The couple stood to say their final goodbyes and to thank everyone for their part in making this a special day for them. Shalan knew it was a birthday she would always remember. She winked at Sheba, who stood holding the wedding bouquet she had caught earlier. Billy had just about broken his neck trying to catch the garter after seeing that Sheba had the bouquet. Everyone had laughed at his eagerness.

They had gotten another wedding surprise the week before. Mother Ingram, her three sons and their wives, Rev. and Mrs. Hampton, and Mother Pearl had chipped in and were sending the couple to Hawaii for a week for their honeymoon. They had protested that it was too much.

"What you two have done for us—a week is not enough. Take it and enjoy," Rev. Hampton told them. Everyone else echoed the sentiment. Not to be outdone, Aunt Faye, LaTia, Tyrese, and Uncle Chip had given them more spending money than they could possibly spend in a week. They were going to spend their wedding night at home and leave for Hawaii the next day. Kendrick was going to spend the night with them and leave for North Carolina the next day with his grandparents. There was a houseful at their house on their wedding night. The family suggested they spend the night at the motel, but this was the way they both wanted things.

"We have the rest of our lives to be together," Levi told his family, "we want to spend some time with you before you go back, and besides, we want Kendrick to be with us our first night together."

Chapter 51

After arriving in Hawaii the next evening, they both took a quick shower. Levi suggested they have dinner and maybe take a walk on the beach. "But first, I want a kiss." He gave her a quick smack.

"That wasn't much of a kiss," Shalan observed.

"What I want more than anything is to make love to you right now. But I know you want to wait and put on one of those little frilly things you women like to wear on your wedding night."

"Oh, is that right?"

"Uh huh."

"What makes you think I brought a 'little frilly thing' with me?"

"Did you?"

"Yes." She walked in his arms and gave him a full kiss on the mouth.

"Okay, how about this?" he whispered close to her ear. "Why don't you go put the little frilly thing on now and we'll eat later?"

"What about the walk on the beach?"

"The beach will be there tomorrow, don't you think?"

"I don't know, it might be."

"Let's take a chance." Shalan got her bag and went in the bathroom to change. Levi took his clothes off and relaxed on the bed in his boxers, flipping through the channels. It had been so long since he had made love to Shalan—and there had been no one since—he hoped he still remembered how.

Shalan looked at herself critically in the mirror. She brushed her hair. She had worn it up for the wedding yesterday, but now it hung down her back the way Levi liked it. She had started to purchase a virginal-looking white negligee, but had opted to buy a sexy purple gown because Levi loved purple. Pleasing him took priority over tradition.

Boy was she nervous. She only hoped that she was able to satisfy him physically. She didn't want to be a huge disappointment to him. She started to open the door, and then went back to the mirror. Maybe I should have gotten the white she second-guessed herself. Oh well, too late now. She slowly opened the door and stood watching Levi.

He looked over and saw her.

"Wow!" She crisscrossed her arms, touching her shoulders, and walked toward the bed. Levi stood up and gently took her hands down. "You look beautiful, you know that?"

"Thank you." He wrapped his arms around her and just held her for a minute. He lowered his head and kissed her. Then sitting on the bed, he pulled her down on his lap.

"Oh, Shalan, I love you so much."

"I love you, too. If I had lost you..." He put his finger to her lips.

"No, baby, we aren't going to talk about the bad times, not tonight. You remember what I told you about this night?"

"No."

"Yes, you do."

"Refresh my memory."

"I told you I was going to make love to you all night long. Remember now?"

"I might remember something like that." Levi gently covered her body with his. This time, after he made love to her, there would be no guilt, no remorse, because it was pleasing to God.

Epilogue

Pastor Levi Leach looked over his congregation at the different faces. He had been pastoring now for almost three years. As soon as the newly formed Male Chorus finished its next selection he would preach an uphill message on *Handling those Valley Experiences*. It was a powerful message that God had given to him in parts. Next week there would be a banquet in his honor and a Pastor appreciation service. He knew it gave the members pleasure to do things like that, but as far as he was concerned, this was happiness—being able to look out and see the growth. The church had grown in numbers. The sanctuary was in the process of being enlarged. More importantly, he could see the spiritual growth.

He and the congregation had been through some good times and some bad times. Through it all, his wife, his beautiful wife, Shalan, had been by his side—the perfect helpmate. He looked at he now holding their daughter, Destiny J'ohnae. His son, Kendrick George Sanders-Leach was sitting proudly beside them, playing the role of the big brother.

He turned his attention back to the Male Chorus. They were singing "My Help" which was the perfect song to go along with his sermon. Sometimes, without him telling him, Billy knew exactly what the choir should sing. Billy and Sheba were his and Shalan's closest friends. They had fun together, yet they respected him as their pastor. Sheba's father had come up and married them a year ago. Levi had been the best man, and Shalan, the matron of honor. They were expecting their first child and celebrating the success of a CD the mass choir had recorded.

Kara and Travis Ingram and their twin toddlers—Travis, Jr. and Tionne—lived down the street from Mother Ingram. Perry and his brothers had remodeled Mother Ingram's house so that there were two master bedrooms downstairs. Mother Davis sold her home and moved in with her. Mother Ingram asked her if she was going to get married and move out like Shalan and Sheba had. Mother Davis had come right back at her and asked, "Are you?"

The hardest service Levi had done since becoming a pastor was the homegoing service for Mother Pearl. KJ had called them six months after their wedding to come to the hospital. The three of them stood around her bed as she told KJ that she was going home to be with the Lord, that she knew he would be okay.

KJ, or Kendrick as he preferred to be called now, had finished his GED and joined the Air Force. He had given the church permission to use the house he grew up in as a halfway house for those who needed help getting on their feet. When he came home next week for the Anniversary celebration, he would stay with Levi and Shalan. It was only after Kendrick was saved that he shared with Levi how deeply in trouble he had been. He knew that if he had kept doing the things he was doing, he would either be locked up now or in a cemetery. He had met someone special while stationed in Texas, and planned to ask her to marry him next Valentine's Day.

Jamal was at Howard University on a full academic scholarship. He was dating but was not in a hurry to get serious. He wanted to complete his education first.

Jalan had finally settled down, gotten his GED, and enrolled in barber school. He was in charge of the nursing home ministry. Just the night before, God had shown Levi that he was calling Jalan to another ministry. He had seen him in a vision preaching the word of God in front of literally thousands of people. Their mother, Jamila, had remarried and she and her husband were active in the church. To her sons' amusement, she had given birth to a baby girl a few months ago. Of course her name started with J, too—Jalisa.

LaTia, known in the modeling world as Ti Ti, could be found on the cover of all the major magazines these days. She promised Tyrese that in a few years she would stop at least long enough to present him with an heir.

Yes, Levi thought, *I have a lot to be thankful for*. Including the fact that Rod and Greg, now both out of college, had relocated to be near him. The two of them were dating identical twins, who were throwing hints about a double church wedding. Delisa and Hugh were expecting their second son. Angie's husband had joined the army and they were stationed in Germany. She had a precious daughter, whom they had only seen pictures of. Pamela, the baby of the family, was in her last year of nursing school. Speaking of nurses—the nurse who had asked Shalan to witness to her was now an active member of Christ's Church. Although her husband hadn't joined, he came with her and their children at least once a month. More recently it had grown to twice a month. Sherise, Shalan's friend from work, had joined the church this year, as had the police officer who had given him CPR. Reggie, the police officer, had attended for a few weeks before joining. He confided in Levi that he wanted to be a part of the church, but there were no other white people there. Levi told him that God was not concerned about skin color, but the condition of souls. He told him the congregation would welcome him with open arms. "However," Levi had told him, "if you feel uncomfortable, find a church with white members, or bring some of your friends here with you." The very next Sunday, Reggie returned with six white friends, two of whom joined with him that very Sunday. Although the other four never came back, the church now had ten white members, including Reggie's fiancée, Roslyn.

It was nothing to look up every few months and see Uncle Chip and his family or Aunt Faye and her new husband come in. LaTia and Tyrese came once a month unless she was on location. Recently Alisa had been making the trip down with them and had talked about moving to Maryland if she could find a good job. Hmmm, Levi thought as he looked over at his drummer, a good job or a good husband? He had seen the two of them talking a lot after service last month. He knew that people joined churches for many different reasons, it was up to him to follow the advice of the Apostle Paul to Timothy: "Do your best to win full approval in God's sight, as a worker who is not ashamed of his work, one who correctly teaches the message of God's truth."

Printed in the United States
25300LVS00001B/247-255

9 781413 755299